a VERY NINJA
CHRISTMAS

ATHENEUM BOOKS FOR YOUNG READERS
An imprint of Simon & Schuster Children's Publishing Division
1230 Avenue of the Americas, New York, New York 10020

For information about special discounts for bulk purchases,
please contact Simon & Schuster Special Sales at 1-866-506-1949
or business@simonandschuster.com.

The Simon & Schuster Speakers Bureau can bring authors
to your live event. For more information or to book an event,
contact the Simon & Schuster Speakers Bureau at 1-866-248-3049 or visit
our website at www.simonspeakers.com.

Book design by Sonia Chaghatzbanian
Manufactured in the United States of America
This Atheneum Books for Young Readers
paperback edition October 2009

2 4 6 8 10 9 7 5 3 1
CIP data for this book is available from the Library of Congress.
ISBN 978-1-4169-8959-2

Jimmy Gownley's

AMELiA RULES! ™

a VERY NINJA CHRISTMAS

Atheneum Books for Young Readers
New York London Toronto Sydney

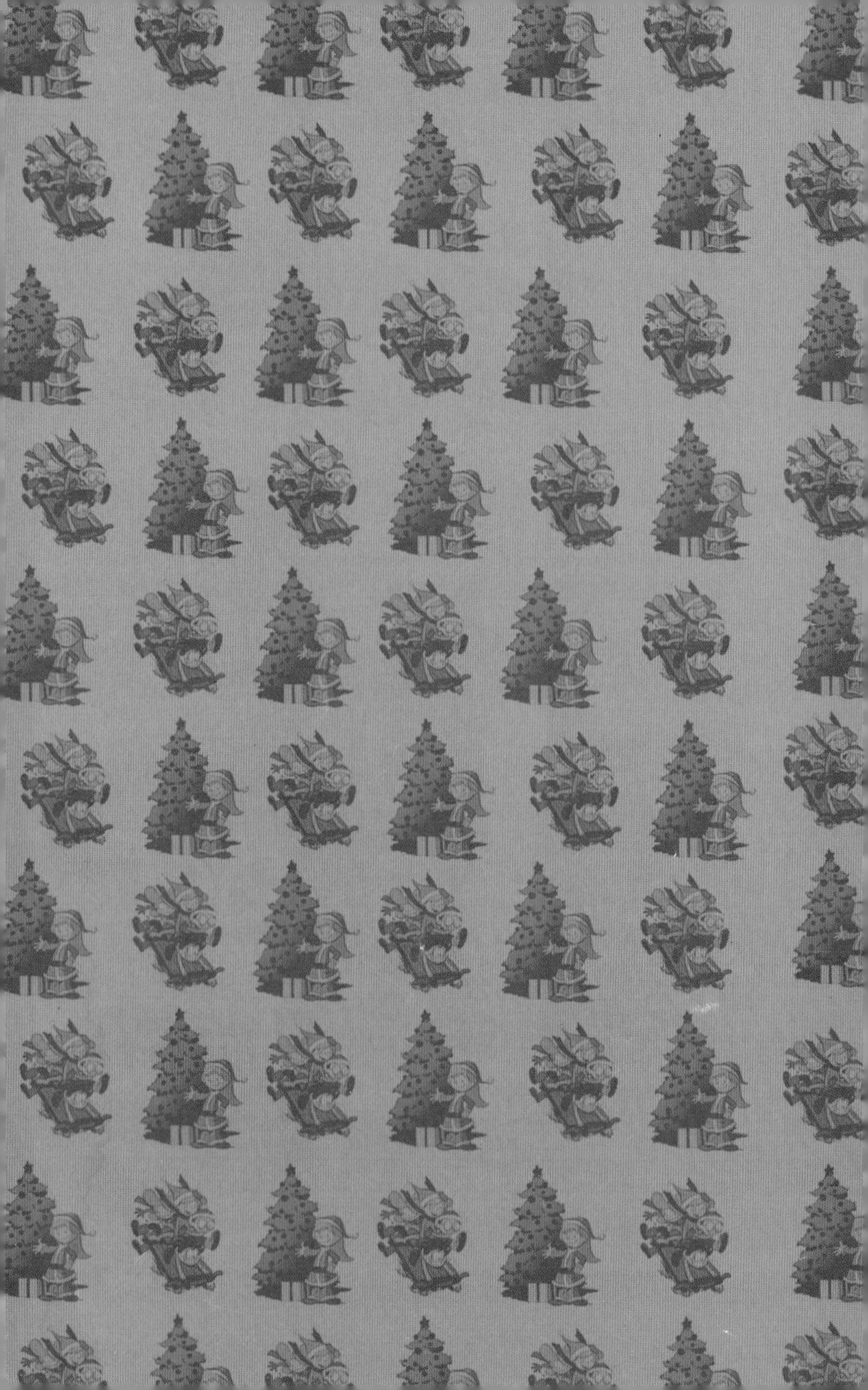

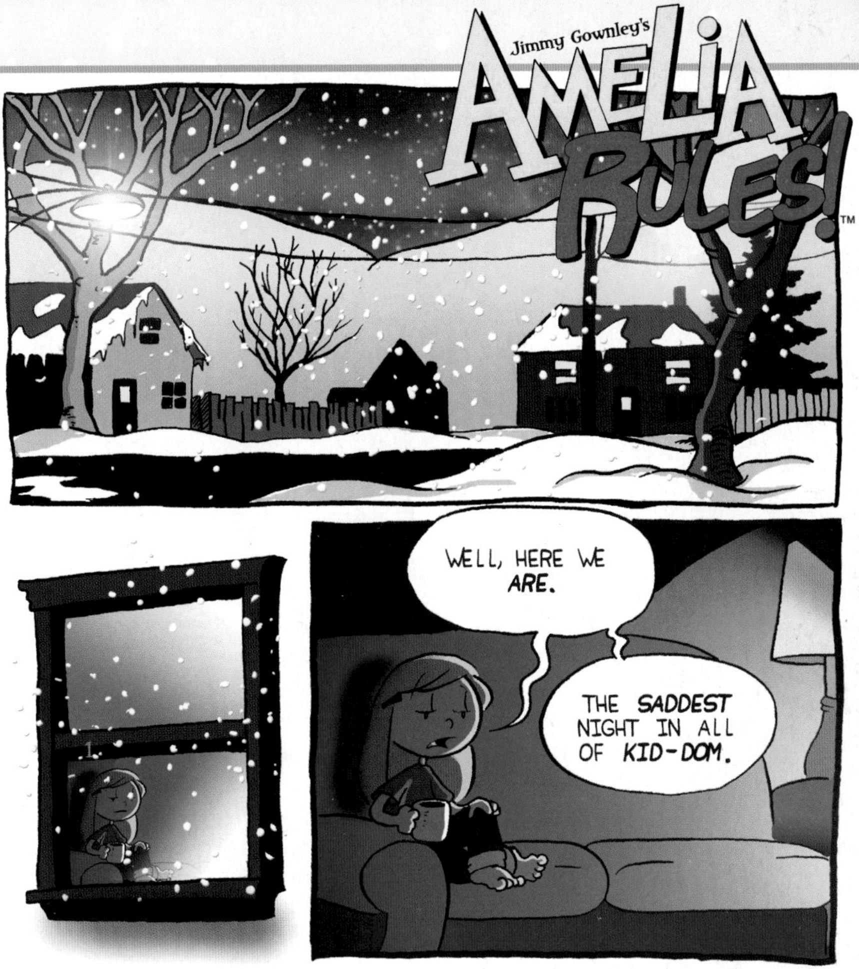
Jimmy Gownley's
AMELIA RULES!
WELL, HERE WE ARE.
THE SADDEST NIGHT IN ALL OF KID-DOM.

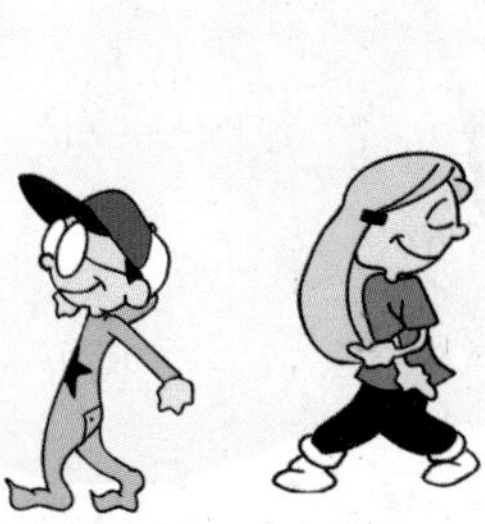

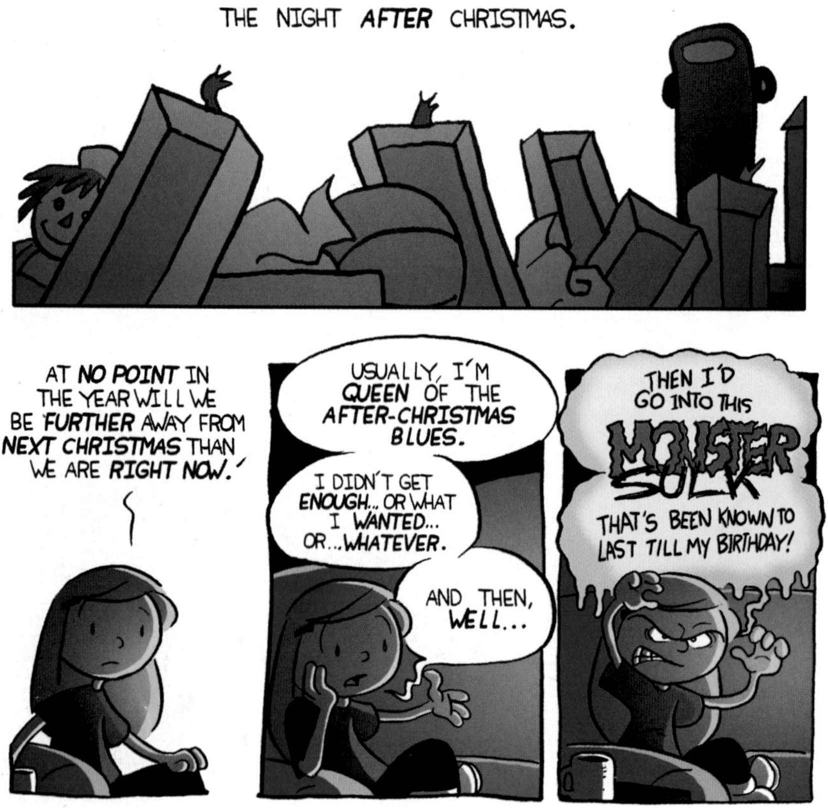
THE NIGHT AFTER CHRISTMAS.
AT NO POINT IN THE YEAR WILL WE BE FURTHER AWAY FROM NEXT CHRISTMAS THAN WE ARE RIGHT NOW.
USUALLY, I'M QUEEN OF THE AFTER-CHRISTMAS BLUES.
I DIDN'T GET ENOUGH... OR WHAT I WANTED... OR... WHATEVER.
AND THEN, WELL...
THEN I'D GO INTO THIS MONSTER SULK THAT'S BEEN KNOWN TO LAST TILL MY BIRTHDAY!

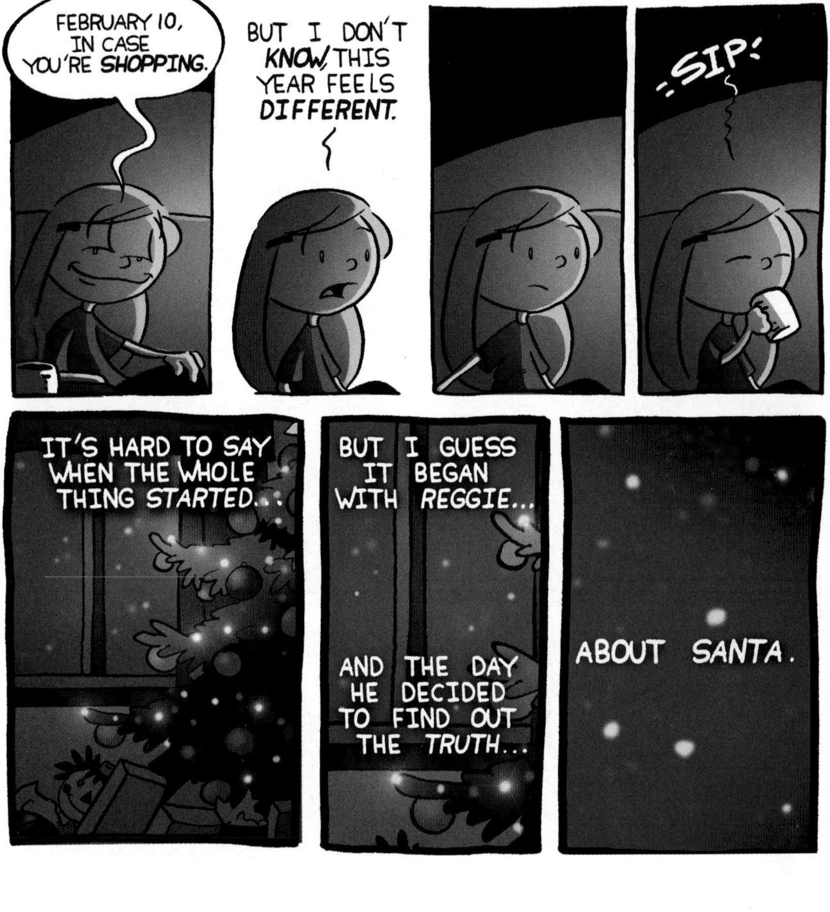
FEBRUARY 10, IN CASE YOU'RE SHOPPING.
BUT I DON'T KNOW, THIS YEAR FEELS DIFFERENT.
SIP!
IT'S HARD TO SAY WHEN THE WHOLE THING STARTED...
BUT I GUESS IT BEGAN WITH REGGIE...
AND THE DAY HE DECIDED TO FIND OUT THE TRUTH...
ABOUT SANTA.

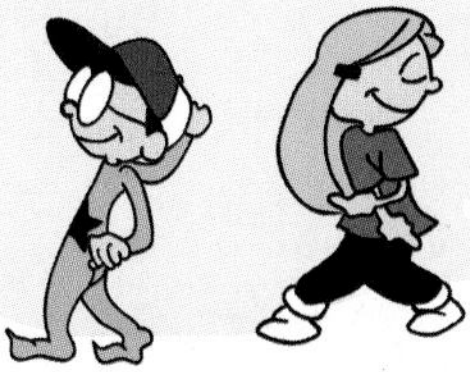

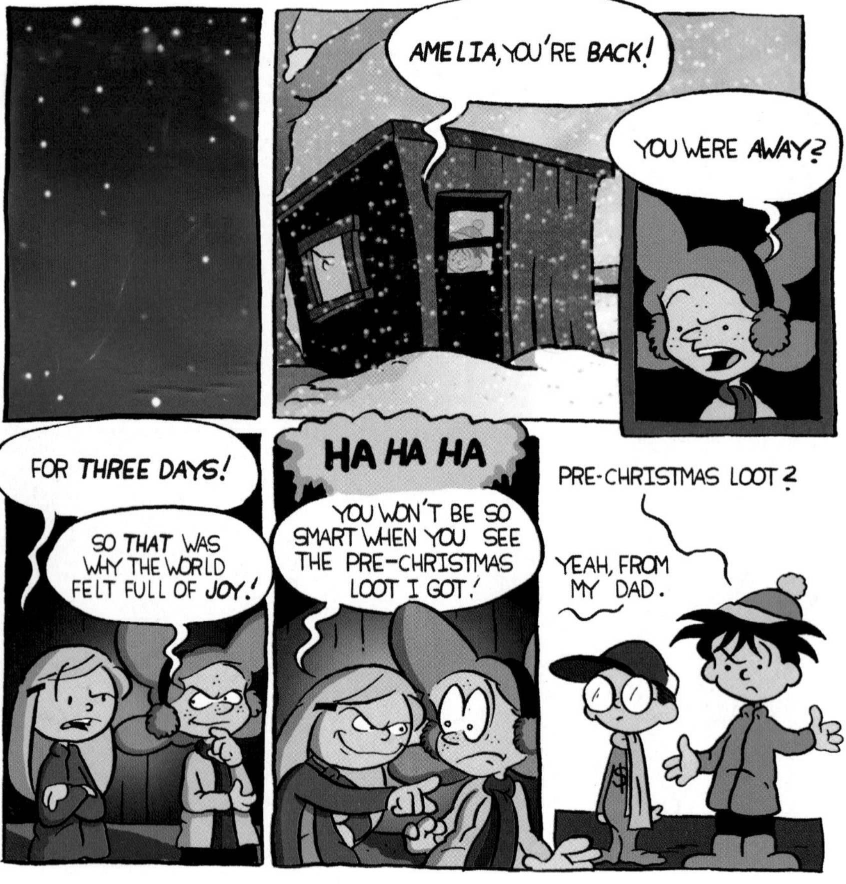
AMELIA, YOU'RE BACK!
YOU WERE AWAY?
FOR THREE DAYS!
SO THAT WAS WHY THE WORLD FELT FULL OF JOY!
HA HA HA
YOU WON'T BE SO SMART WHEN YOU SEE THE PRE-CHRISTMAS LOOT I GOT!
PRE-CHRISTMAS LOOT?
YEAH, FROM MY DAD.

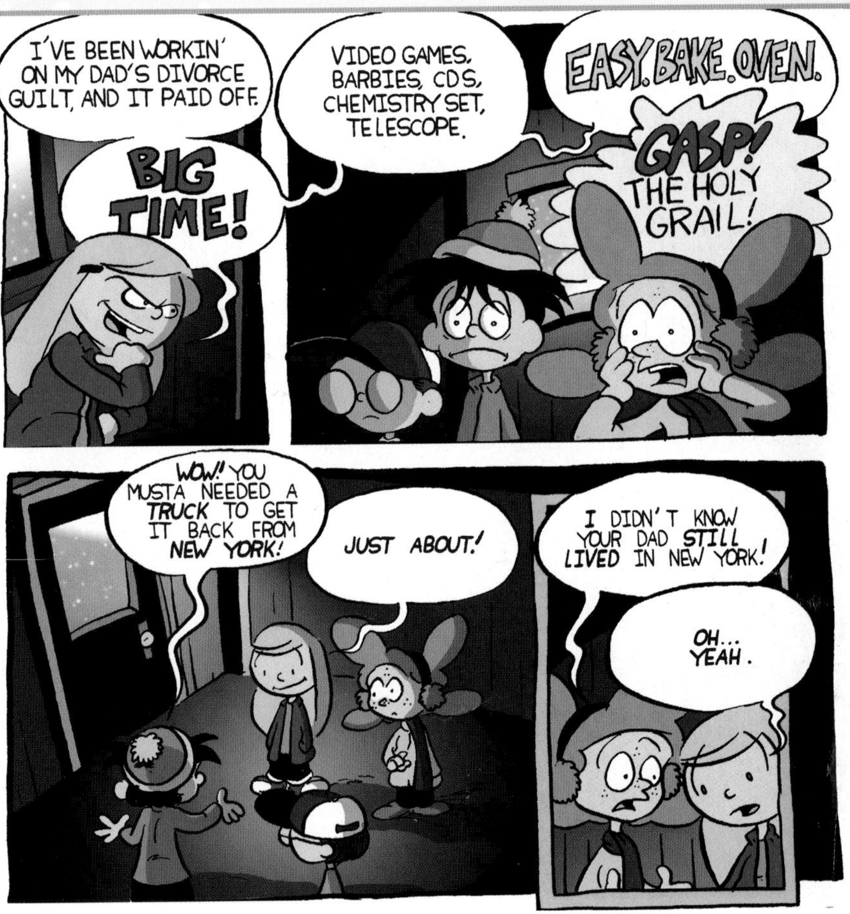
I'VE BEEN WORKIN' ON MY DAD'S DIVORCE GUILT, AND IT PAID OFF.
BIG TIME!
VIDEO GAMES, BARBIES, CDS, CHEMISTRY SET, TELESCOPE.
EASY. BAKE. OVEN.
GASP! THE HOLY GRAIL!
WOW! YOU MUSTA NEEDED A TRUCK TO GET IT BACK FROM NEW YORK!
JUST ABOUT!
I DIDN'T KNOW YOUR DAD STILL LIVED IN NEW YORK!
OH... YEAH.

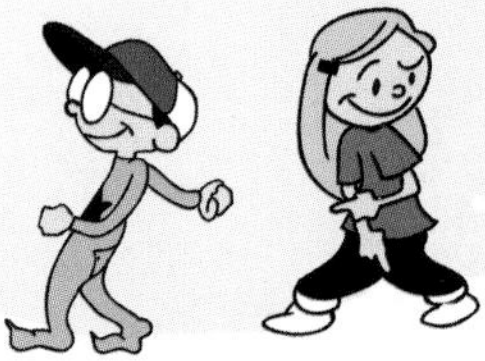

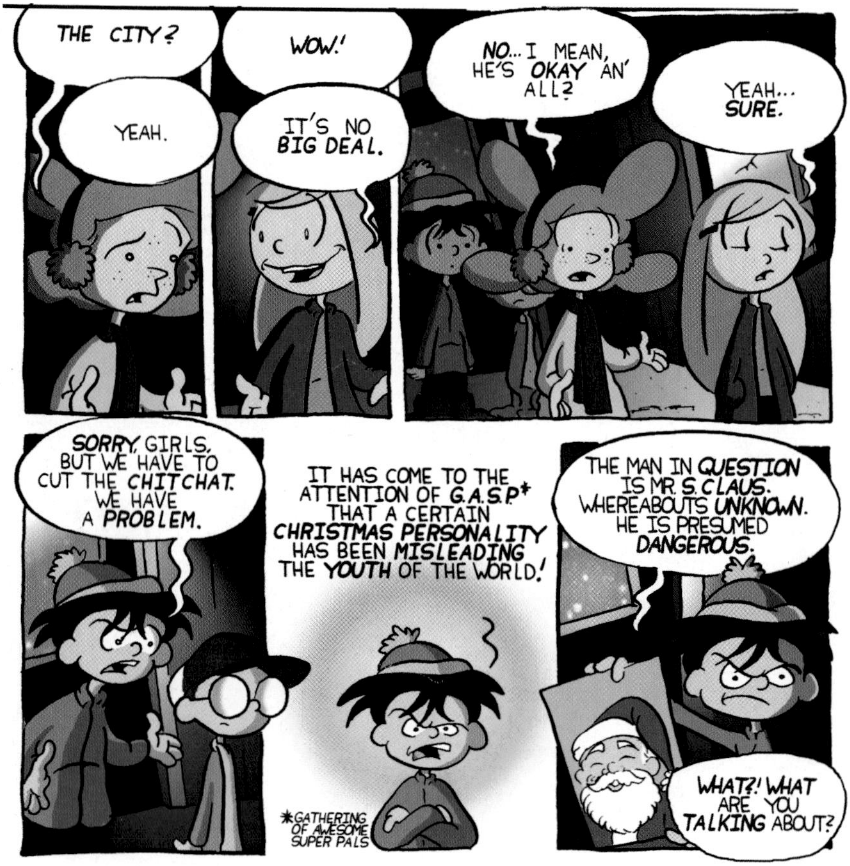
THE CITY?
YEAH.
WOW!
IT'S NO BIG DEAL.
NO... I MEAN, HE'S OKAY AN' ALL?
YEAH... SURE.
SORRY, GIRLS, BUT WE HAVE TO CUT THE CHITCHAT. WE HAVE A PROBLEM.
IT HAS COME TO THE ATTENTION OF G.A.S.P* THAT A CERTAIN CHRISTMAS PERSONALITY HAS BEEN MISLEADING THE YOUTH OF THE WORLD!
*GATHERING OF AWESOME SUPER PALS
THE MAN IN QUESTION IS MR. S. CLAUS. WHEREABOUTS UNKNOWN. HE IS PRESUMED DANGEROUS.
WHAT?! WHAT ARE YOU TALKING ABOUT?

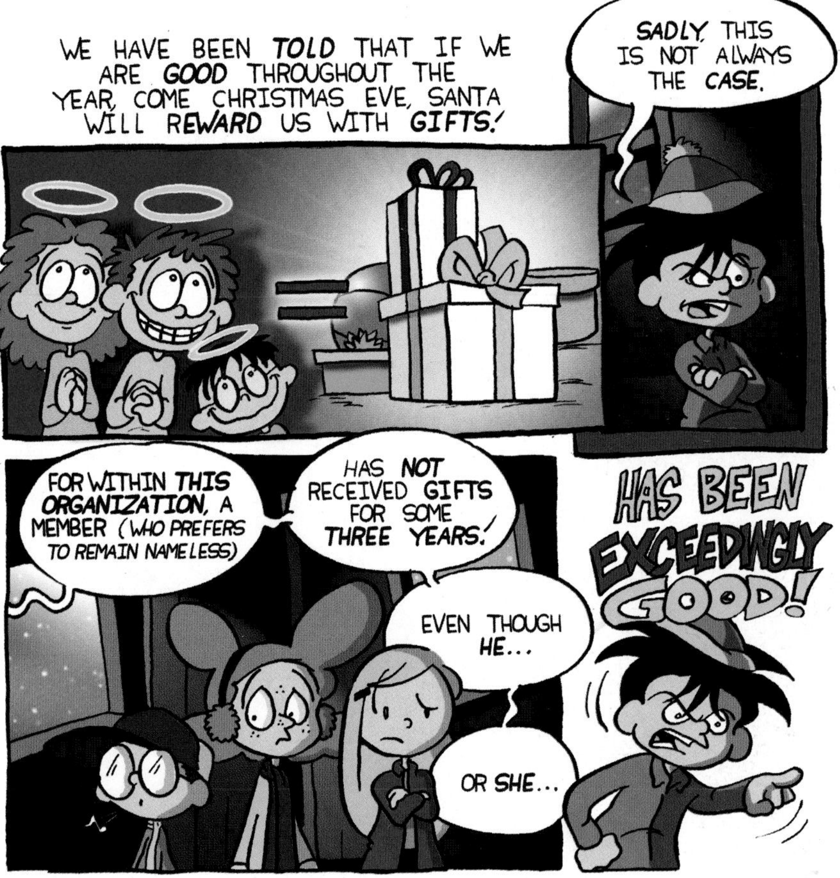
WE HAVE BEEN TOLD THAT IF WE ARE GOOD THROUGHOUT THE YEAR, COME CHRISTMAS EVE, SANTA WILL REWARD US WITH GIFTS!
SADLY, THIS IS NOT ALWAYS THE CASE.
FOR WITHIN THIS ORGANIZATION, A MEMBER (WHO PREFERS TO REMAIN NAMELESS)
HAS NOT RECEIVED GIFTS FOR SOME THREE YEARS!
EVEN THOUGH HE...
OR SHE...
HAS BEEN EXCEEDINGLY GOOD!

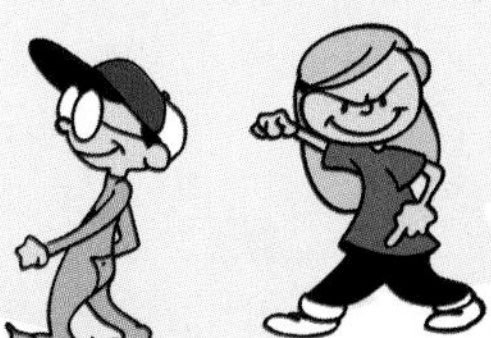

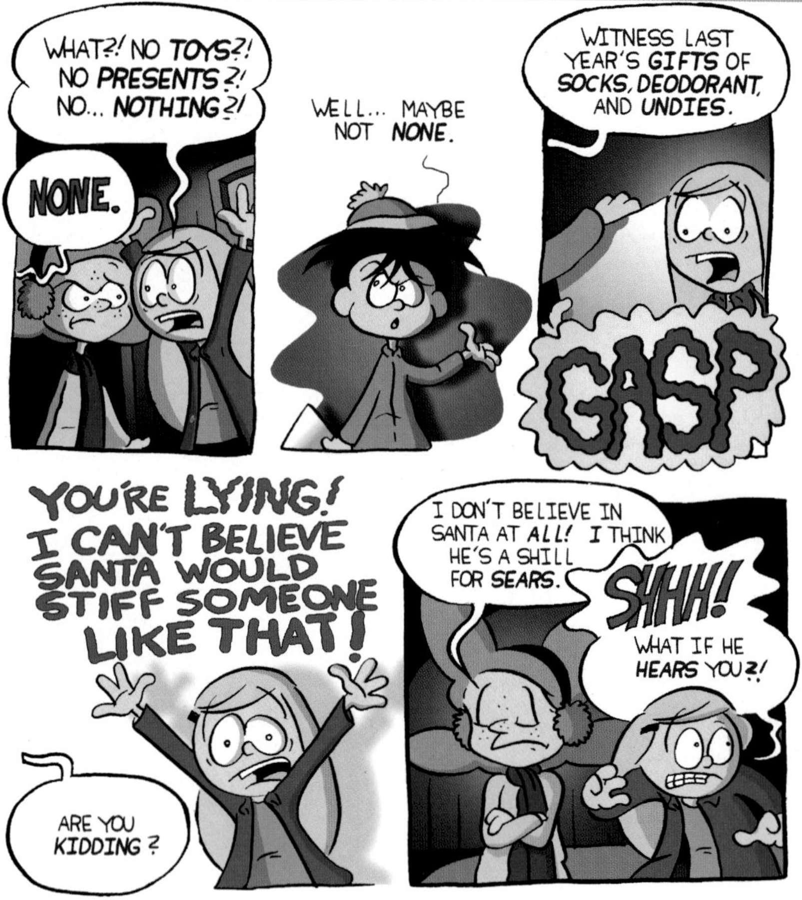
WHAT?! NO TOYS?! NO PRESENTS?! NO... NOTHING?!
NONE.
WELL... MAYBE NOT NONE.
WITNESS LAST YEAR'S GIFTS OF SOCKS, DEODORANT, AND UNDIES.
GASP
YOU'RE LYING! I CAN'T BELIEVE SANTA WOULD STIFF SOMEONE LIKE THAT!
ARE YOU KIDDING?
I DON'T BELIEVE IN SANTA AT ALL! I THINK HE'S A SHILL FOR SEARS.
SHHH! WHAT IF HE HEARS YOU?!

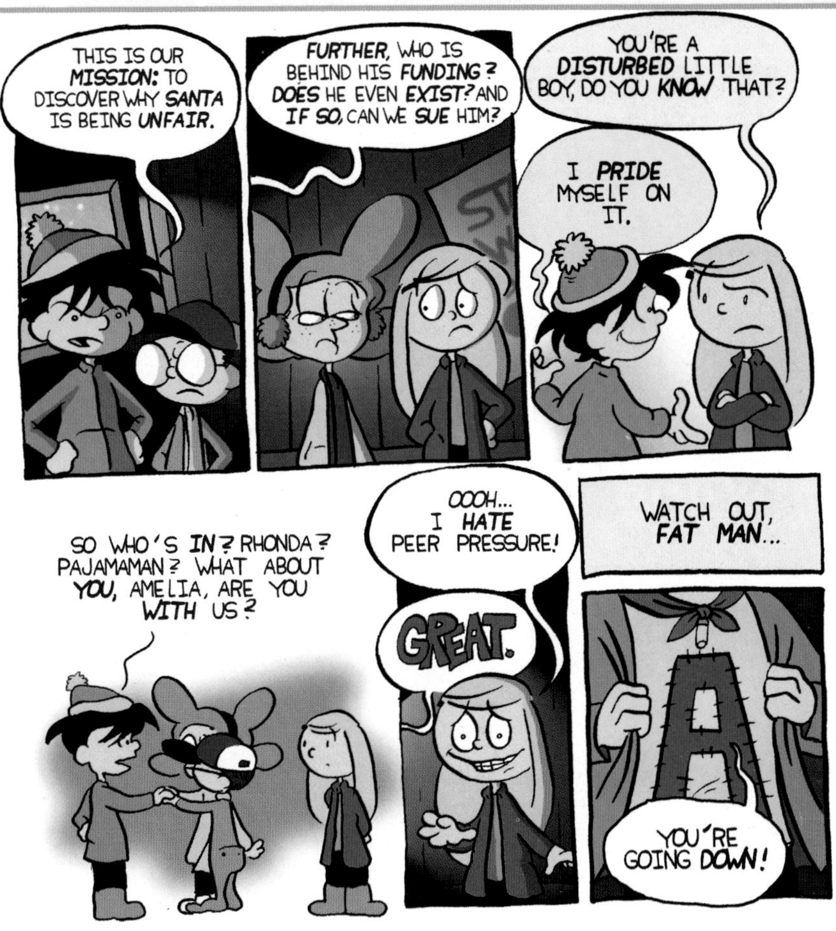
THIS IS OUR MISSION: TO DISCOVER WHY SANTA IS BEING UNFAIR.
FURTHER, WHO IS BEHIND HIS FUNDING? DOES HE EVEN EXIST? AND IF SO, CAN WE SUE HIM?
YOU'RE A DISTURBED LITTLE BOY, DO YOU KNOW THAT?
I PRIDE MYSELF ON IT.
SO WHO'S IN? RHONDA? PAJAMAMAN? WHAT ABOUT YOU, AMELIA, ARE YOU WITH US?
OOOH... I HATE PEER PRESSURE!
GREAT.
WATCH OUT, FAT MAN...
YOU'RE GOING DOWN!

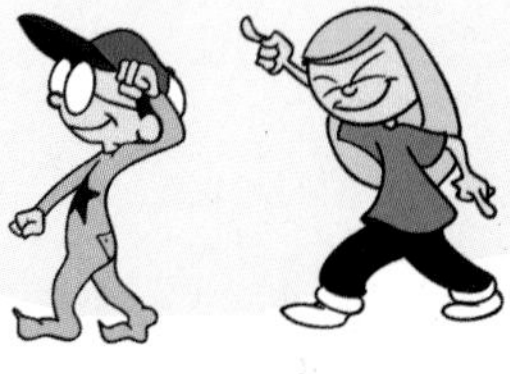

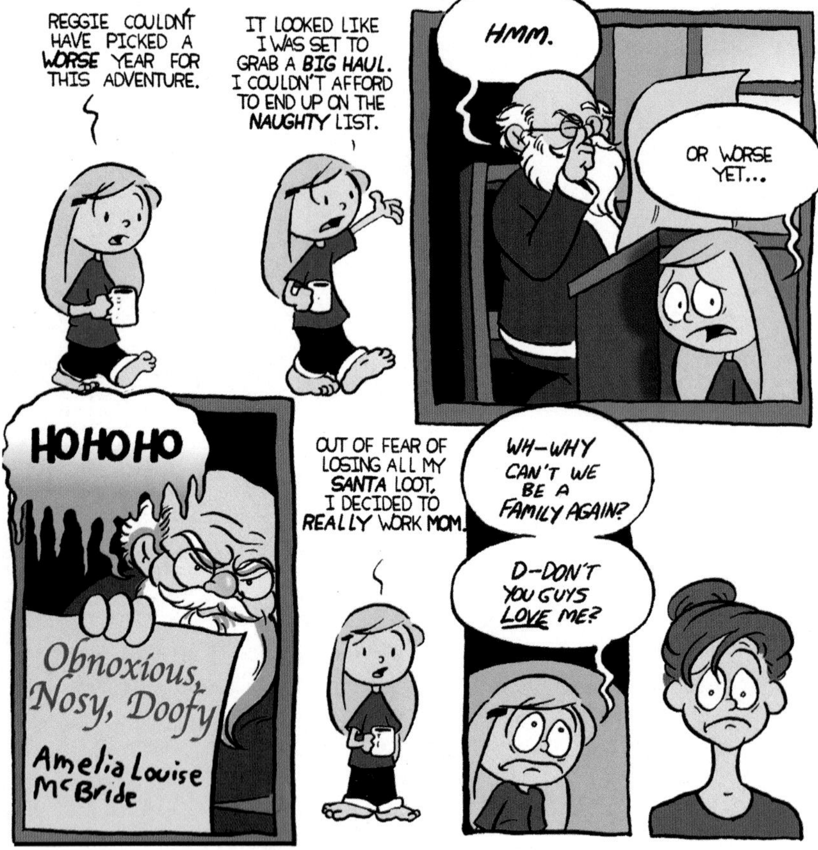
REGGIE COULDN'T HAVE PICKED A WORSE YEAR FOR THIS ADVENTURE.
IT LOOKED LIKE I WAS SET TO GRAB A BIG HAUL. I COULDN'T AFFORD TO END UP ON THE NAUGHTY LIST.
HMM.
OR WORSE YET...
HOHOHO
Obnoxious, Nosy, Doofy
Amelia Louise McBride
OUT OF FEAR OF LOSING ALL MY SANTA LOOT, I DECIDED TO REALLY WORK MOM.
WH-WHY CAN'T WE BE A FAMILY AGAIN?
D-DON'T YOU GUYS LOVE ME?

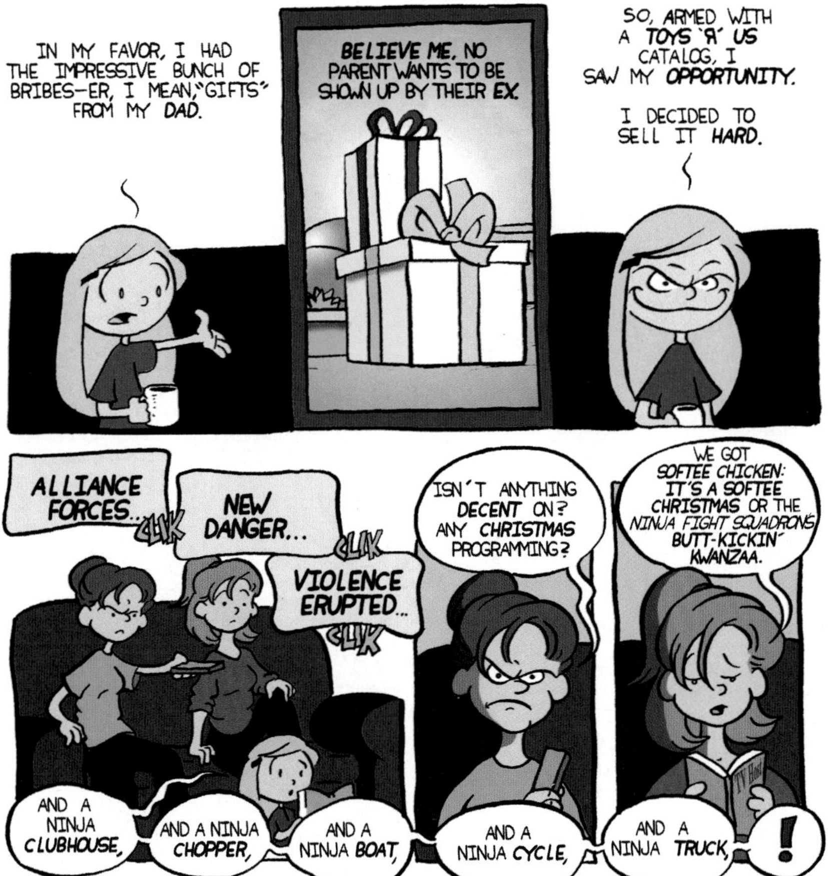
IN MY FAVOR, I HAD THE IMPRESSIVE BUNCH OF BRIBES—ER, I MEAN, "GIFTS" FROM MY DAD.
BELIEVE ME, NO PARENT WANTS TO BE SHOWN UP BY THEIR EX.
SO, ARMED WITH A TOYS 'R' US CATALOG, I SAW MY OPPORTUNITY.
I DECIDED TO SELL IT HARD.
ALLIANCE FORCES...
CLIK
NEW DANGER...
CLIK
VIOLENCE ERUPTED...
CLIK
ISN'T ANYTHING DECENT ON? ANY CHRISTMAS PROGRAMMING?
WE GOT SOFTEE CHICKEN: IT'S A SOFTEE CHRISTMAS OR THE NINJA FIGHT SQUADRONS BUTT-KICKIN' KWANZAA.
TV Host
AND A NINJA CLUBHOUSE,
AND A NINJA CHOPPER,
AND A NINJA BOAT,
AND A NINJA CYCLE,
AND A NINJA TRUCK,
!

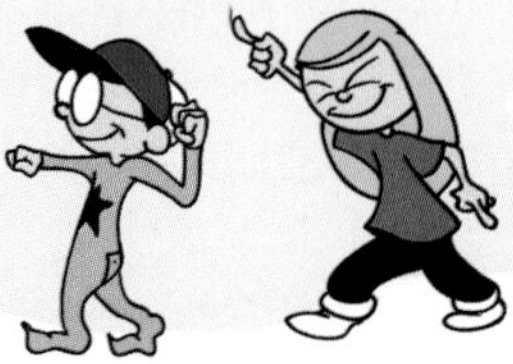

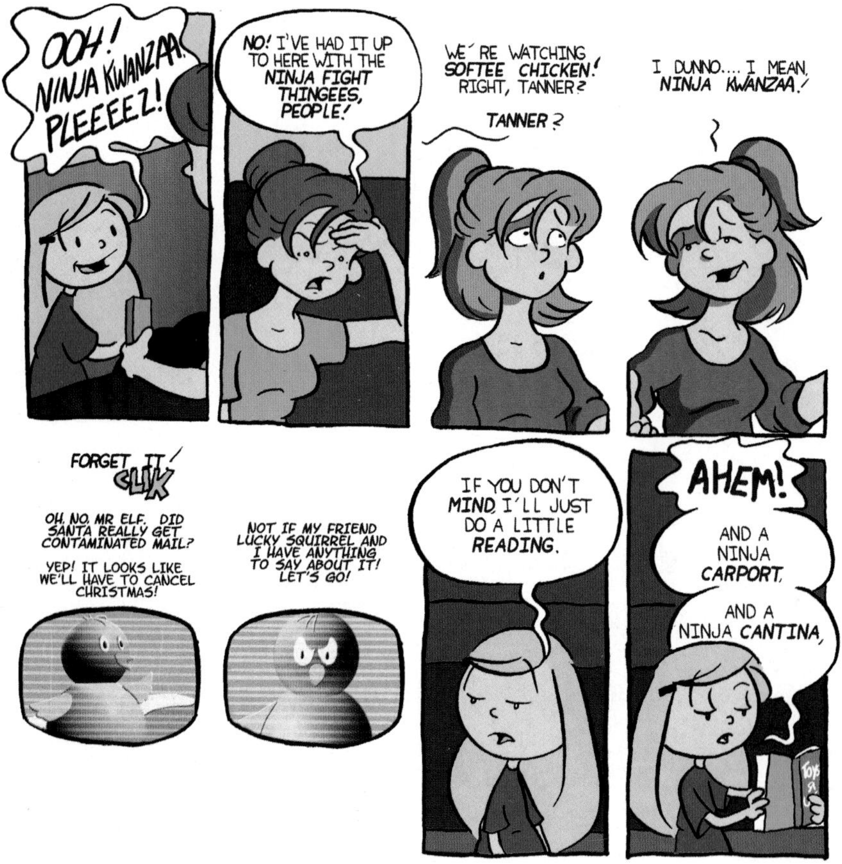
OOH! NINJA KWANZAA! PLEEEEZ!
NO! I'VE HAD IT UP TO HERE WITH THE NINJA FIGHT THINGEES, PEOPLE!
WE'RE WATCHING SOFTEE CHICKEN! RIGHT, TANNER?
TANNER?
I DUNNO.... I MEAN, NINJA KWANZAA!
FORGET IT!
CLIK
OH, NO, MR ELF. DID SANTA REALLY GET CONTAMINATED MAIL?
YEP! IT LOOKS LIKE WE'LL HAVE TO CANCEL CHRISTMAS!
NOT IF MY FRIEND LUCKY SQUIRREL AND I HAVE ANYTHING TO SAY ABOUT IT! LET'S GO!
IF YOU DON'T MIND, I'LL JUST DO A LITTLE READING.
AHEM!
AND A NINJA CARPORT,
AND A NINJA CANTINA,

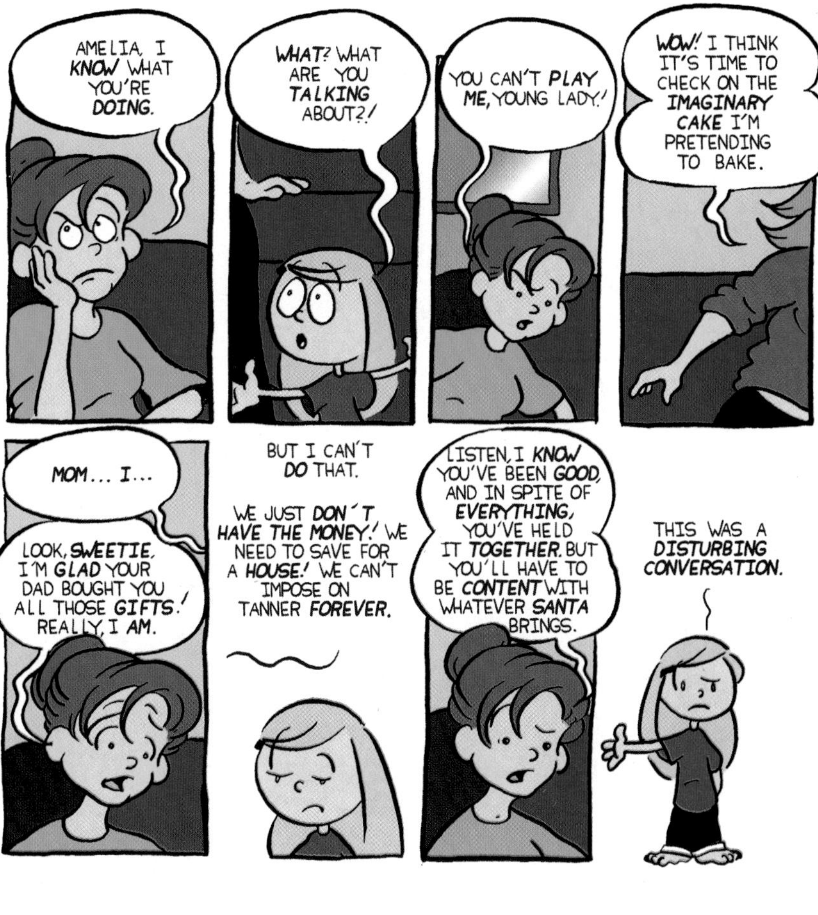
AMELIA, I KNOW WHAT YOU'RE DOING.
WHAT? WHAT ARE YOU TALKING ABOUT?!
YOU CAN'T PLAY ME, YOUNG LADY!
WOW! I THINK IT'S TIME TO CHECK ON THE IMAGINARY CAKE I'M PRETENDING TO BAKE.
MOM... I...
LOOK, SWEETIE, I'M GLAD YOUR DAD BOUGHT YOU ALL THOSE GIFTS! REALLY, I AM.
BUT I CAN'T DO THAT.
WE JUST DON'T HAVE THE MONEY! WE NEED TO SAVE FOR A HOUSE! WE CAN'T IMPOSE ON TANNER FOREVER.
LISTEN, I KNOW YOU'VE BEEN GOOD, AND IN SPITE OF EVERYTHING, YOU'VE HELD IT TOGETHER. BUT YOU'LL HAVE TO BE CONTENT WITH WHATEVER SANTA BRINGS.
THIS WAS A DISTURBING CONVERSATION.

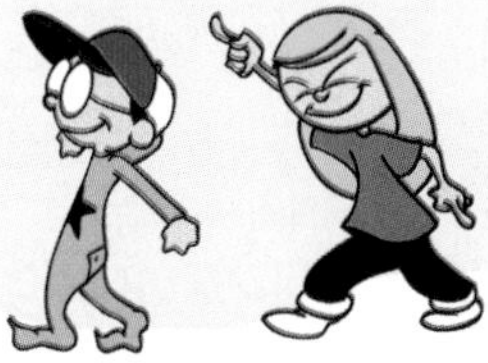

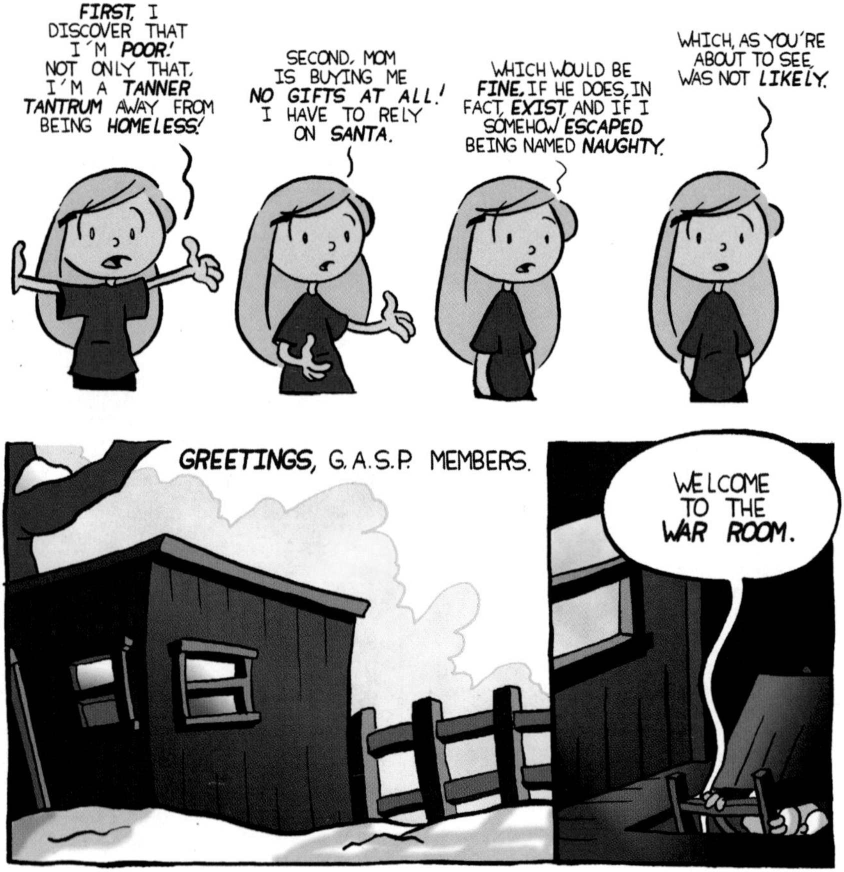
FIRST, I DISCOVER THAT I'M POOR! NOT ONLY THAT, I'M A TANNER TANTRUM AWAY FROM BEING HOMELESS!
SECOND, MOM IS BUYING ME NO GIFTS AT ALL! I HAVE TO RELY ON SANTA.
WHICH WOULD BE FINE, IF HE DOES, IN FACT, EXIST, AND IF I SOMEHOW ESCAPED BEING NAMED NAUGHTY.
WHICH, AS YOU'RE ABOUT TO SEE, WAS NOT LIKELY.
GREETINGS, G.A.S.P. MEMBERS.
WELCOME TO THE WAR ROOM.

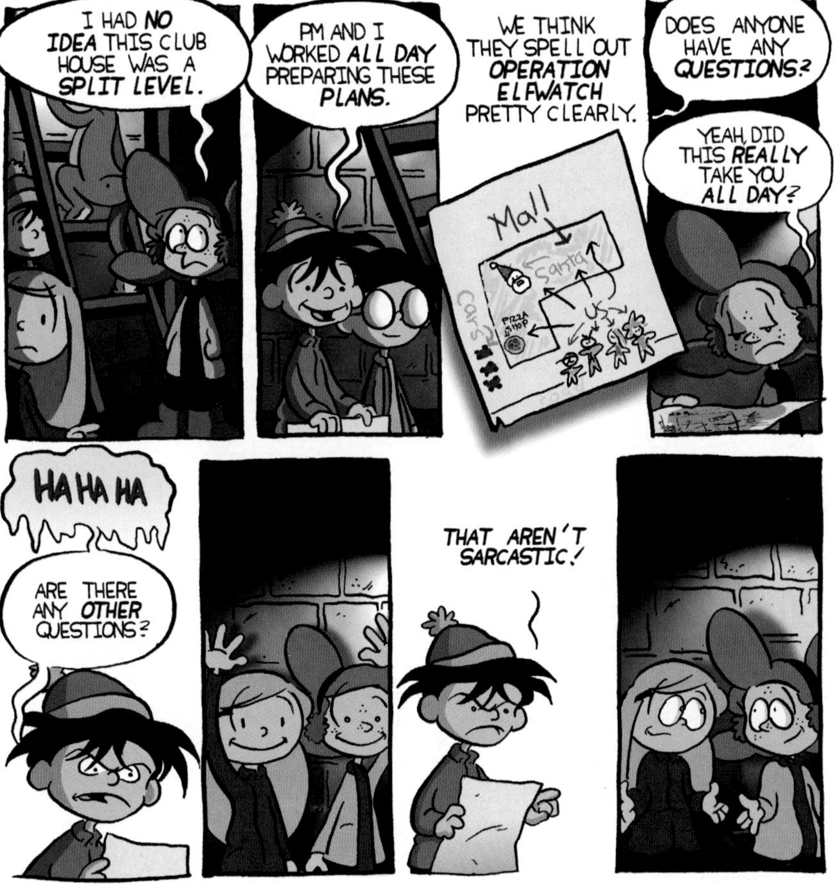
I HAD **NO IDEA** THIS CLUB HOUSE WAS A **SPLIT LEVEL.**
PM AND I WORKED **ALL DAY** PREPARING THESE **PLANS.**
WE THINK THEY SPELL OUT **OPERATION ELFWATCH** PRETTY CLEARLY.
Mall
Santa
Cars
PIZZA SHOP
US
DOES ANYONE HAVE ANY **QUESTIONS?**
YEAH, DID THIS **REALLY** TAKE YOU **ALL DAY?**
HA HA HA
ARE THERE ANY **OTHER** QUESTIONS?
THAT AREN'T SARCASTIC!

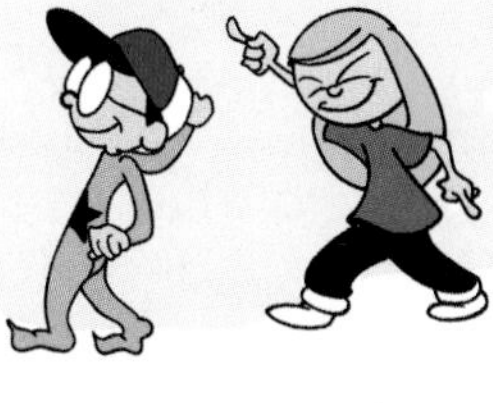

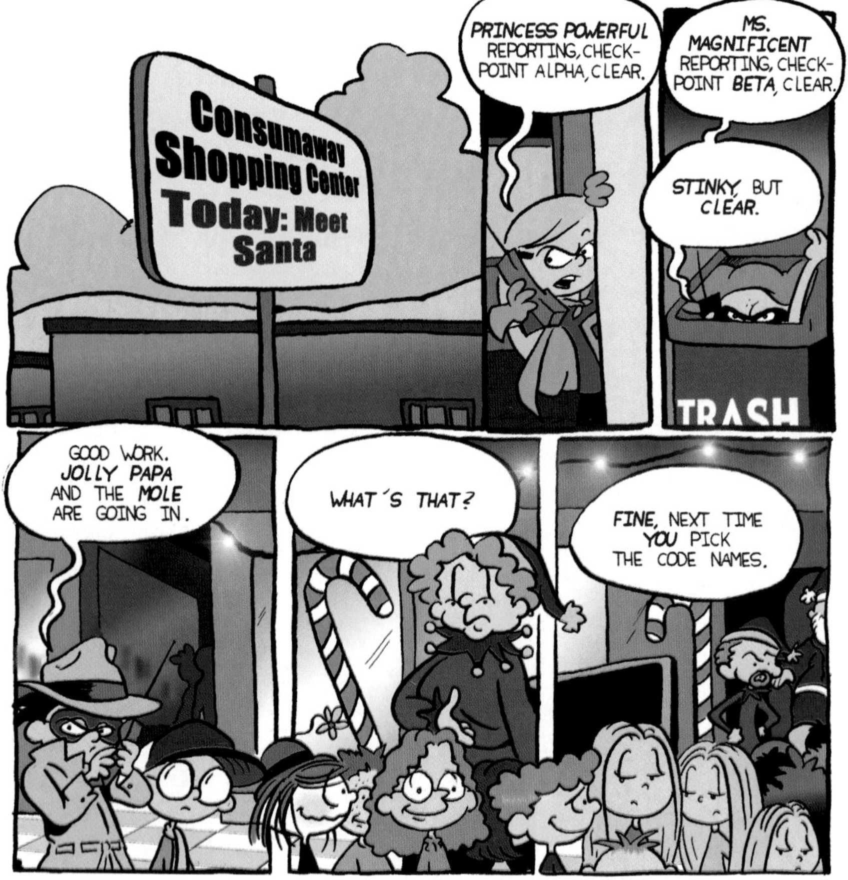
Consumaway Shopping Center Today: Meet Santa
PRINCESS POWERFUL REPORTING, CHECK-POINT ALPHA, CLEAR.
MS. MAGNIFICENT REPORTING, CHECK-POINT BETA, CLEAR.
STINKY, BUT CLEAR.
TRASH
GOOD WORK. JOLLY PAPA AND THE MOLE ARE GOING IN.
WHAT'S THAT?
FINE, NEXT TIME YOU PICK THE CODE NAMES.

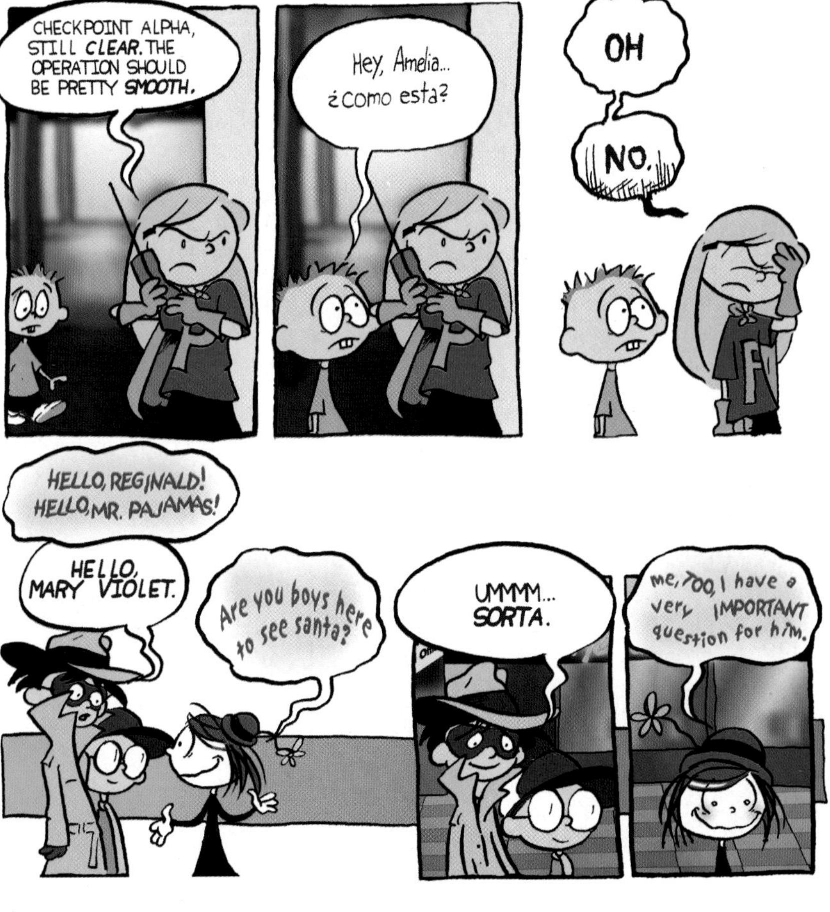
CHECKPOINT ALPHA, STILL CLEAR. THE OPERATION SHOULD BE PRETTY SMOOTH.
Hey, Amelia... ¿como esta?
OH
NO.
HELLO, REGINALD! HELLO, MR. PAJAMAS!
HELLO, MARY VIOLET.
Are you boys here to see santa?
UMMMM... SORTA.
me, TOO, I have a very IMPORTANT question for him.

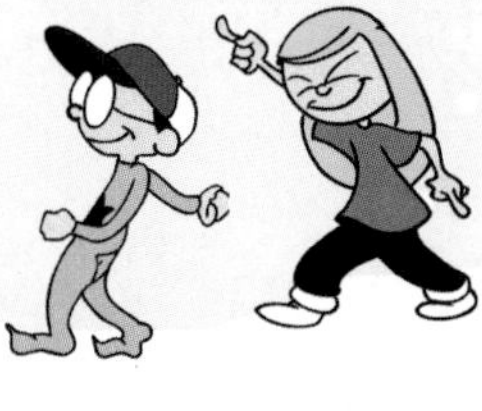

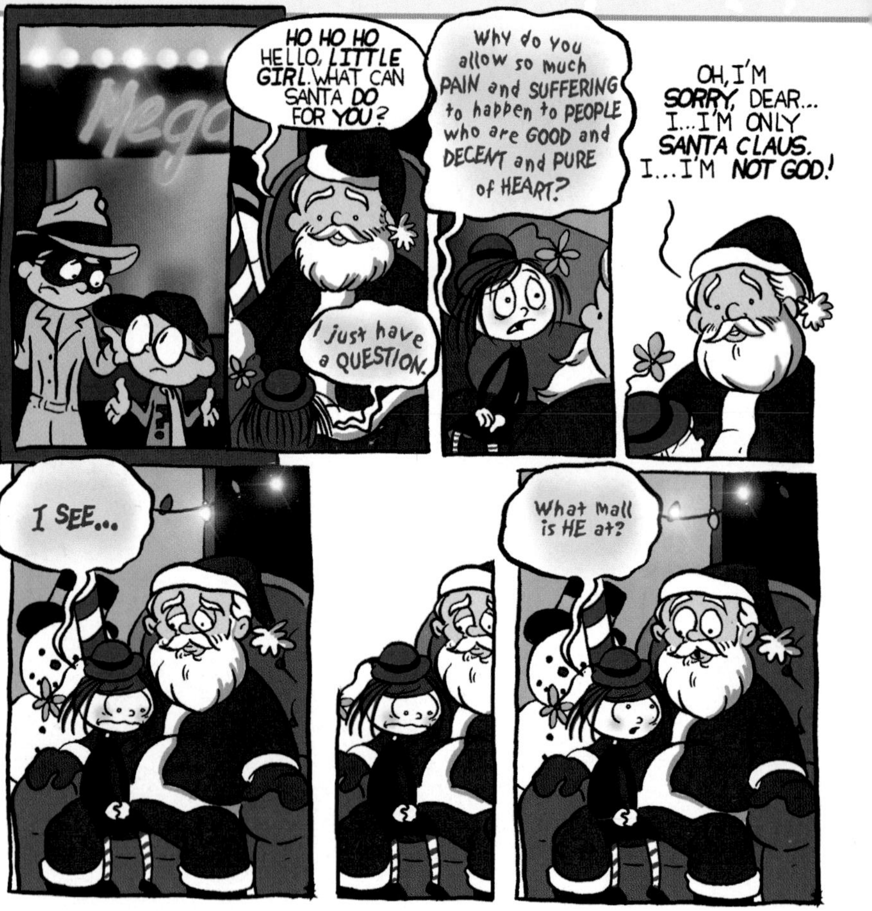
HO HO HO HELLO, LITTLE GIRL. WHAT CAN SANTA DO FOR YOU?
I just have a QUESTION.
Why do you allow so much PAIN and SUFFERING to happen to PEOPLE who are GOOD and DECENT and PURE of HEART?
OH, I'M SORRY, DEAR... I...I'M ONLY SANTA CLAUS. I...I'M NOT GOD!
I SEE...
What mall is HE at?

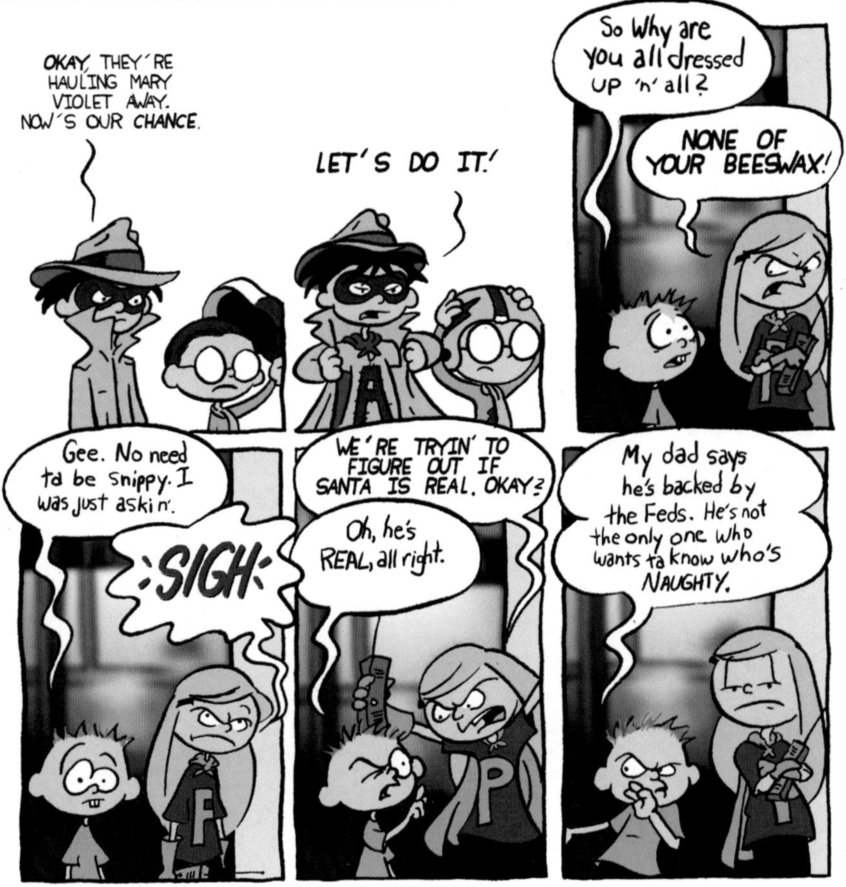
OKAY, THEY'RE HAULING MARY VIOLET AWAY. NOW'S OUR CHANCE.
LET'S DO IT!
So why are you all dressed up 'n' all?
NONE OF YOUR BEESWAX!
Gee. No need ta be snippy. I was just askin'.
SIGH
WE'RE TRYIN' TO FIGURE OUT IF SANTA IS REAL. OKAY?
Oh, he's REAL, all right.
My dad says he's backed by the Feds. He's not the only one who wants ta know who's NAUGHTY.

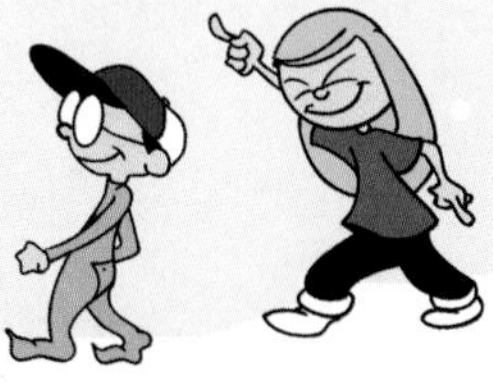

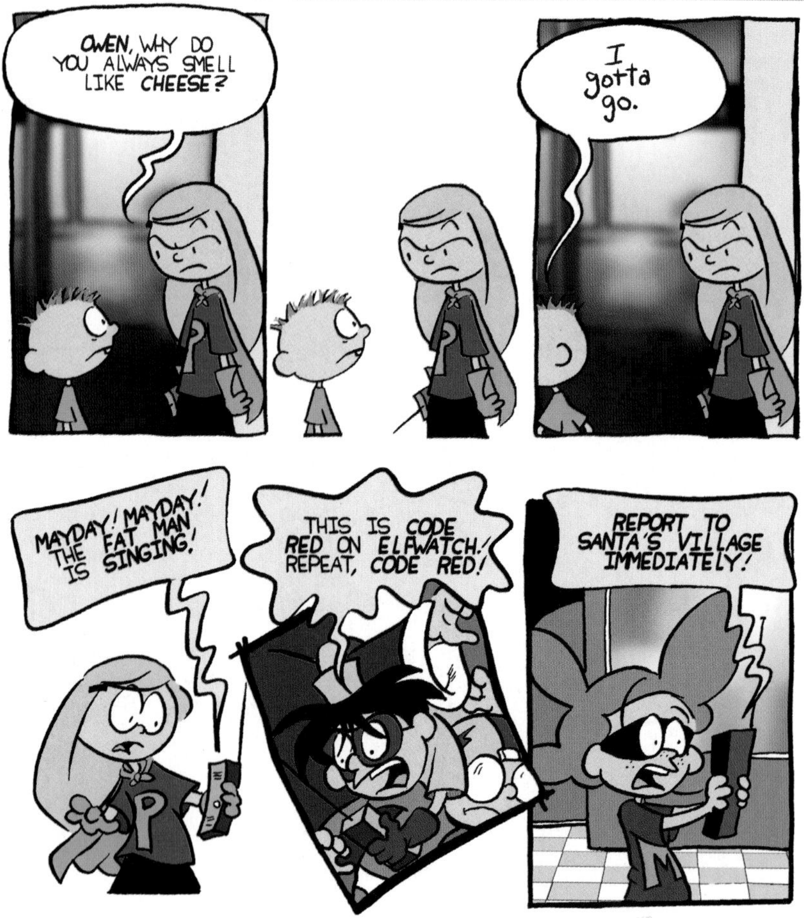
OWEN, WHY DO YOU ALWAYS SMELL LIKE CHEESE?
I gotta go.
MAYDAY! MAYDAY! THE FAT MAN IS SINGING!
THIS IS CODE RED ON ELFWATCH! REPEAT, CODE RED!
REPORT TO SANTA'S VILLAGE IMMEDIATELY!

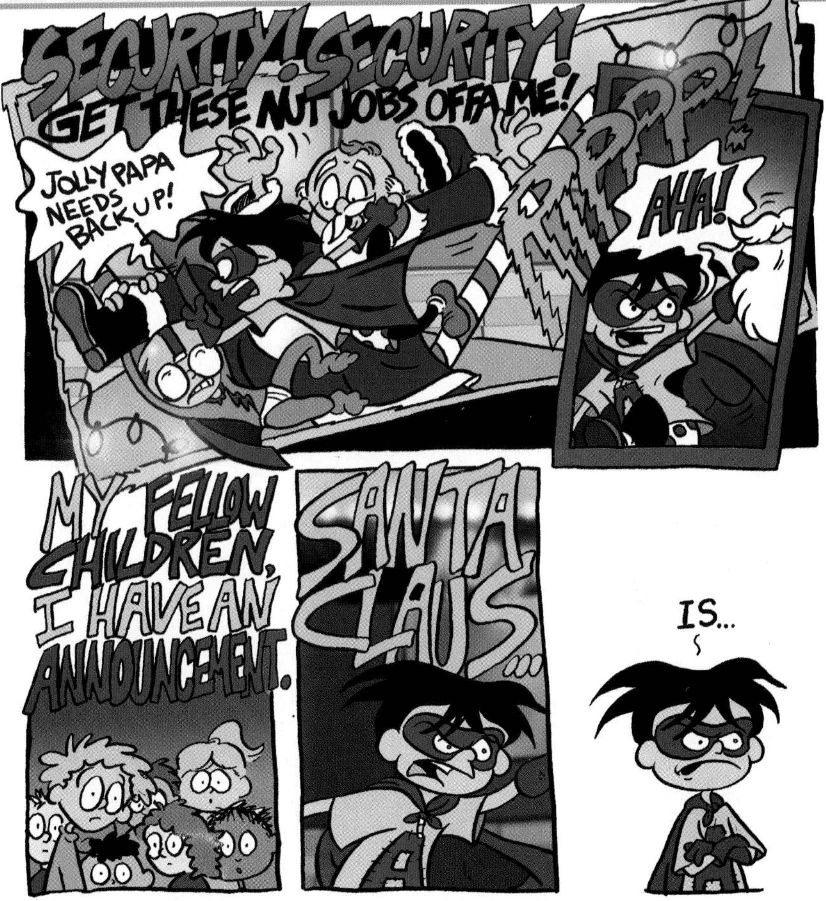
SECURITY! SECURITY! GET THESE NUT JOBS OFFA ME!
JOLLY PAPA NEEDS BACKUP!
AHA!
MY FELLOW CHILDREN, I HAVE AN ANNOUNCEMENT.
SANTA CLAUS...
IS...

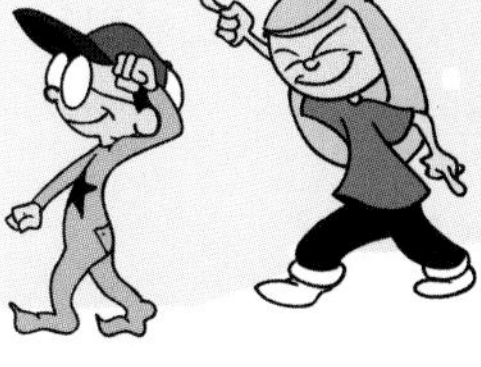

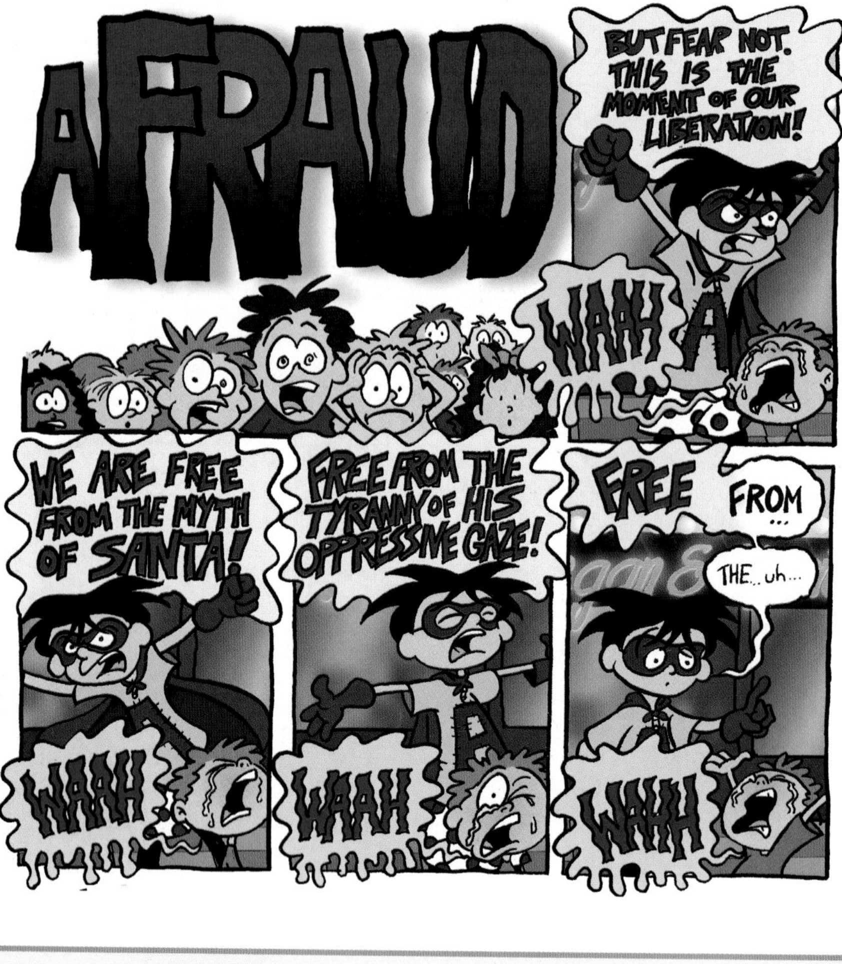
A FRAUD
BUT FEAR NOT. THIS IS THE MOMENT OF OUR LIBERATION!
WAAH
WE ARE FREE FROM THE MYTH OF SANTA!
WAAH
FREE FROM THE TYRANNY OF HIS OPPRESSIVE GAZE!
WAAH
FREE
FROM ...
THE... uh...
WAHH

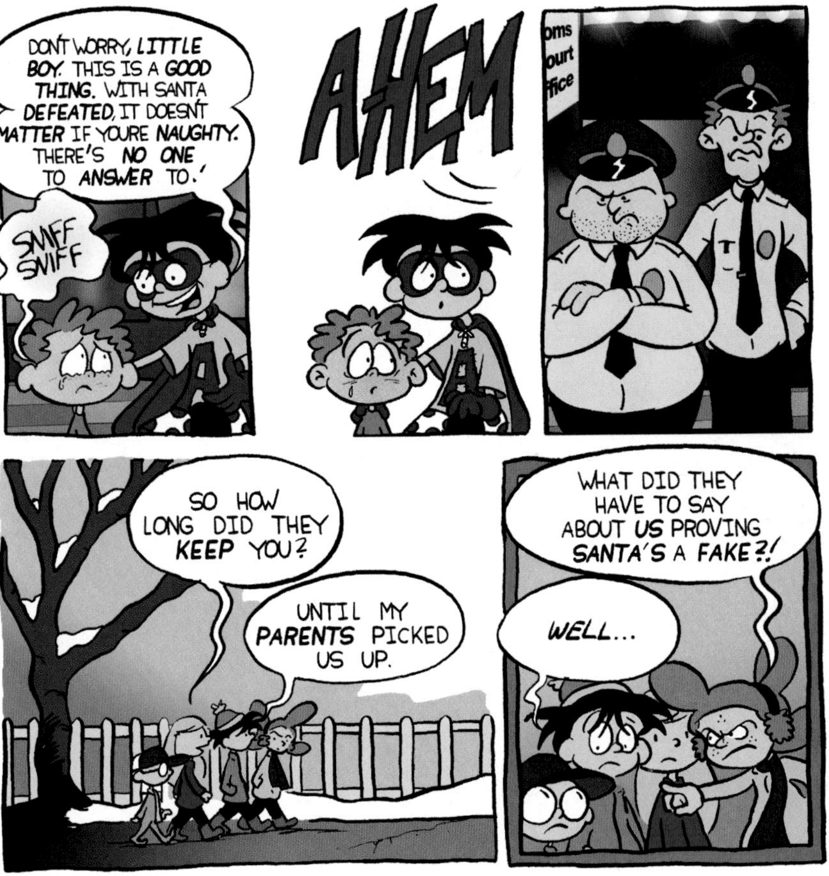
DON'T WORRY, LITTLE BOY. THIS IS A GOOD THING. WITH SANTA DEFEATED, IT DOESN'T MATTER IF YOU'RE NAUGHTY. THERE'S NO ONE TO ANSWER TO.
SNIFF SNIFF
AHEM
SO HOW LONG DID THEY KEEP YOU?
UNTIL MY PARENTS PICKED US UP.
WHAT DID THEY HAVE TO SAY ABOUT US PROVING SANTA'S A FAKE?!
WELL...

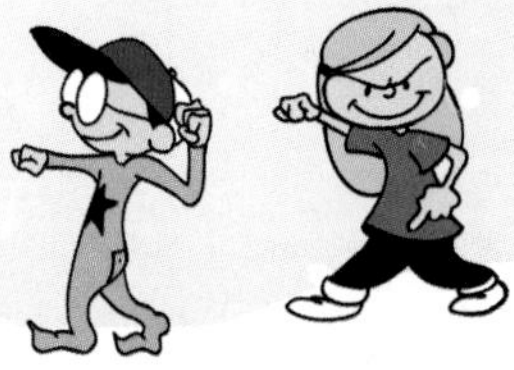

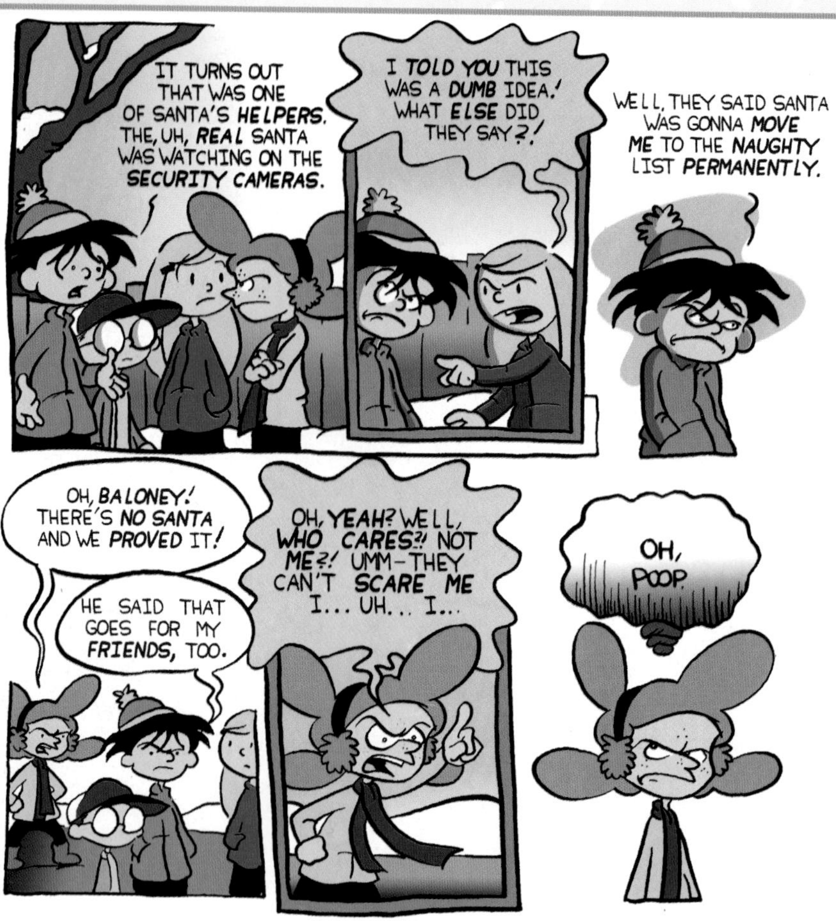
IT TURNS OUT THAT WAS ONE OF SANTA'S HELPERS. THE, UH, REAL SANTA WAS WATCHING ON THE SECURITY CAMERAS.
I TOLD YOU THIS WAS A DUMB IDEA! WHAT ELSE DID THEY SAY?!
WELL, THEY SAID SANTA WAS GONNA MOVE ME TO THE NAUGHTY LIST PERMANENTLY.
OH, BALONEY! THERE'S NO SANTA AND WE PROVED IT!
HE SAID THAT GOES FOR MY FRIENDS, TOO.
OH, YEAH? WELL, WHO CARES?! NOT ME?! UMM–THEY CAN'T SCARE ME I... UH... I...
OH, POOP.

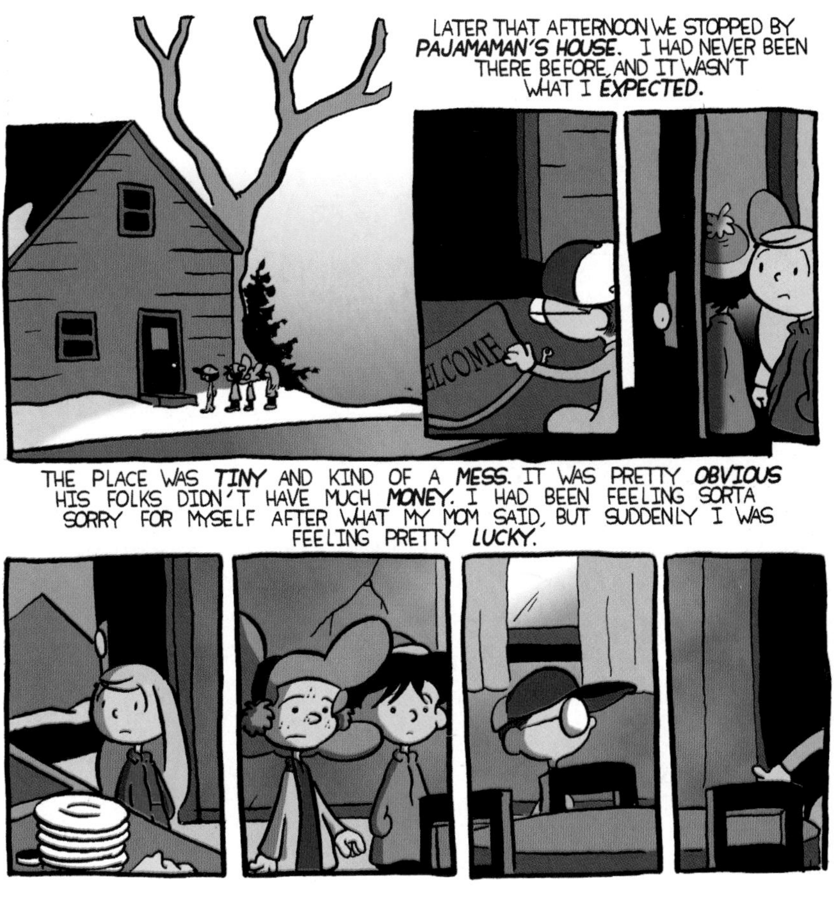
LATER THAT AFTERNOON WE STOPPED BY **PAJAMAMAN'S HOUSE**. I HAD NEVER BEEN THERE BEFORE, AND IT WASN'T WHAT I **EXPECTED**.
ELCOME
THE PLACE WAS **TINY** AND KIND OF A **MESS**. IT WAS PRETTY **OBVIOUS** HIS FOLKS DIDN'T HAVE MUCH **MONEY**. I HAD BEEN FEELING SORTA SORRY FOR MYSELF AFTER WHAT MY MOM SAID, BUT SUDDENLY I WAS FEELING PRETTY **LUCKY**.

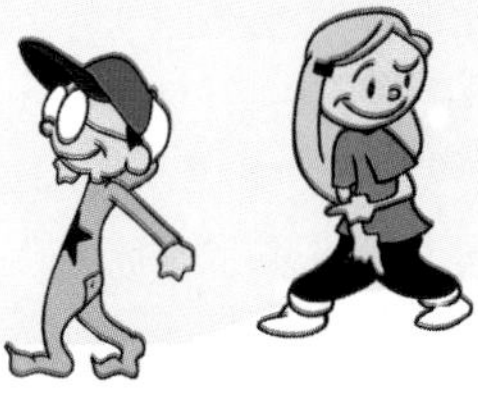

WHILE PM WAS OUT OF THE ROOM, I NOTICED THIS **CLIPPING** FROM A CATALOG TAPED TO THE FRIDGE. IT CAUGHT MY EYE CUZ IT WAS FOR THE ***RED CAPTAIN NINJA*** THAT WAS AT THE TOP OF ***MY*** WANT LIST. I REALLY THOUGHT DAD WOULD ***COME THROUGH*** WITH IT, BUT I GUESS THEY'RE PRETTY HARD TO FIND.

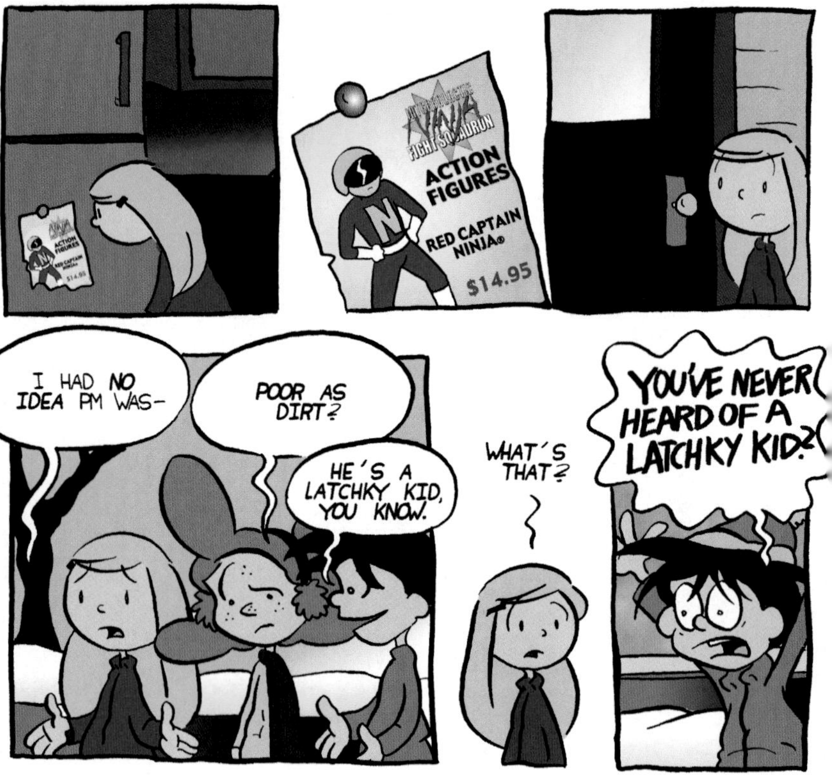

NINJA
FIGHT SQUADRON
ACTION FIGURES
RED CAPTAIN NINJA®
$14.95
I HAD NO IDEA PM WAS-
POOR AS DIRT?
HE'S A LATCHKY KID, YOU KNOW.
WHAT'S THAT?
YOU'VE NEVER HEARD OF A LATCHKY KID?

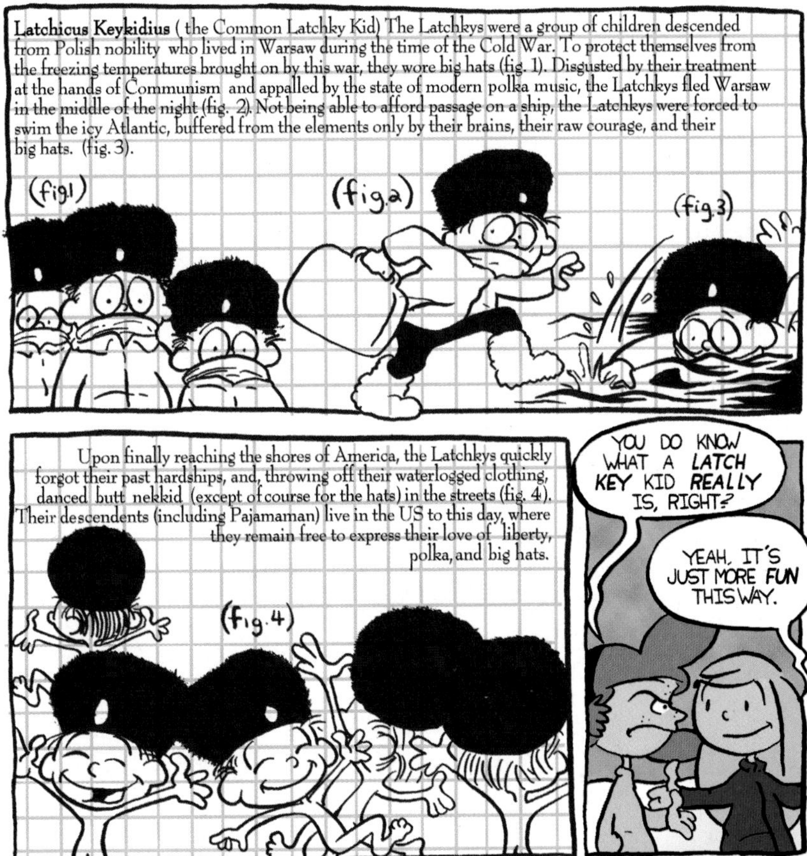
Latchicus Keykidius (the Common Latchky Kid) The Latchkys were a group of children descended from Polish nobility who lived in Warsaw during the time of the Cold War. To protect themselves from the freezing temperatures brought on by this war, they wore big hats (fig. 1). Disgusted by their treatment at the hands of Communism and appalled by the state of modern polka music, the Latchkys fled Warsaw in the middle of the night (fig. 2). Not being able to afford passage on a ship, the Latchkys were forced to swim the icy Atlantic, buffered from the elements only by their brains, their raw courage, and their big hats. (fig. 3).
(fig.1)
(fig.2)
(fig.3)
Upon finally reaching the shores of America, the Latchkys quickly forgot their past hardships, and, throwing off their waterlogged clothing, danced butt nekkid (except of course for the hats) in the streets (fig. 4). Their descendents (including Pajamaman) live in the US to this day, where they remain free to express their love of liberty, polka, and big hats.
(fig.4)
YOU DO KNOW WHAT A **LATCH KEY** KID **REALLY** IS, RIGHT?
YEAH, IT'S JUST MORE **FUN** THIS WAY.

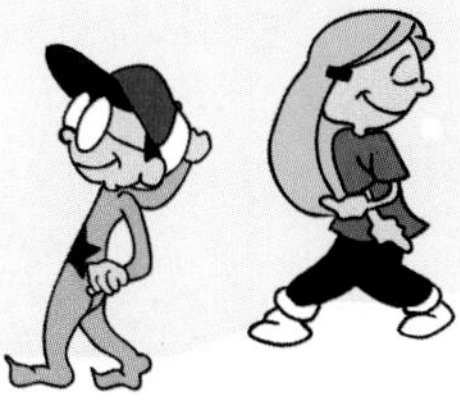

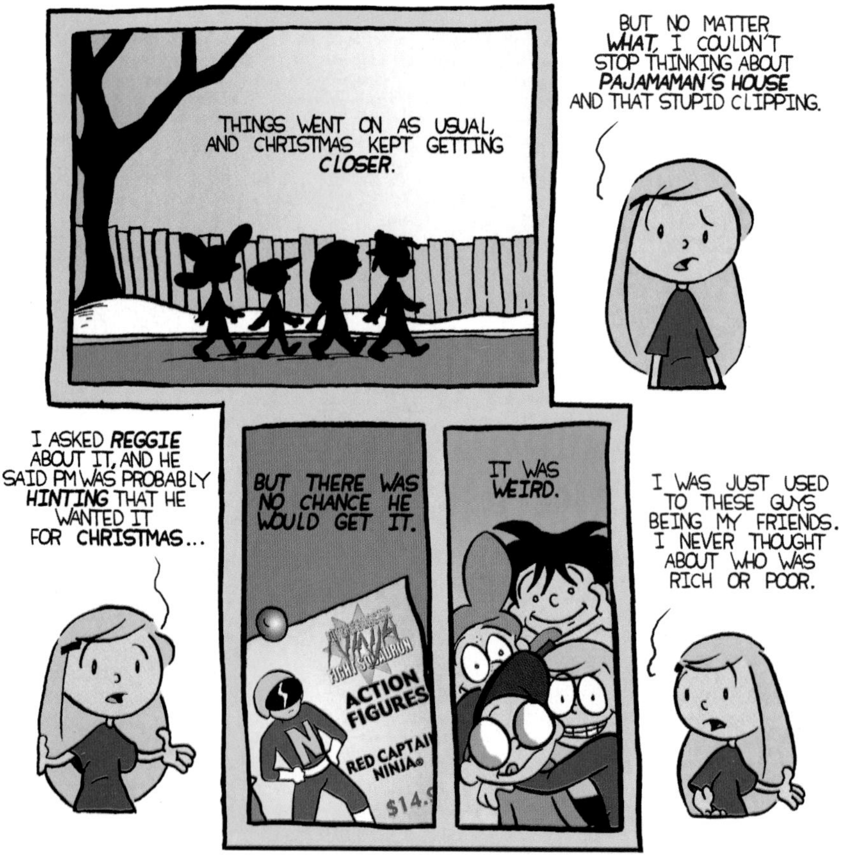
THINGS WENT ON AS USUAL, AND CHRISTMAS KEPT GETTING CLOSER.
BUT NO MATTER WHAT, I COULDN'T STOP THINKING ABOUT PAJAMAMAN'S HOUSE AND THAT STUPID CLIPPING.
I ASKED REGGIE ABOUT IT, AND HE SAID PM WAS PROBABLY HINTING THAT HE WANTED IT FOR CHRISTMAS...
BUT THERE WAS NO CHANCE HE WOULD GET IT.
ACTION FIGURES
RED CAPTAIN NINJA®
IT WAS WEIRD.
I WAS JUST USED TO THESE GUYS BEING MY FRIENDS. I NEVER THOUGHT ABOUT WHO WAS RICH OR POOR.

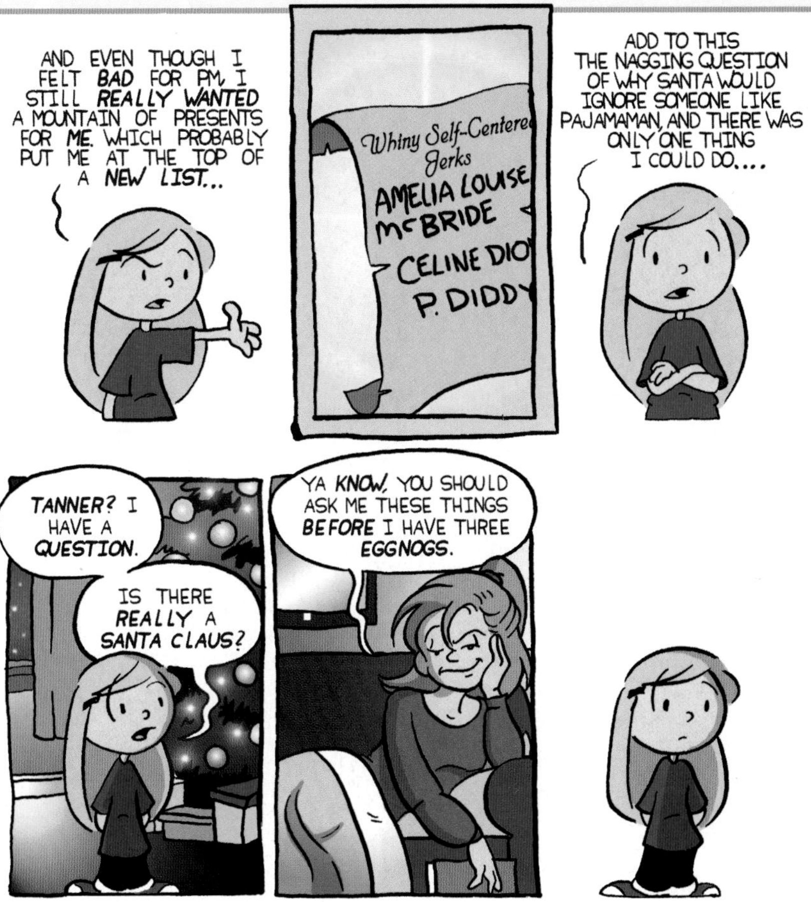
AND EVEN THOUGH I FELT BAD FOR PM, I STILL REALLY WANTED A MOUNTAIN OF PRESENTS FOR ME. WHICH PROBABLY PUT ME AT THE TOP OF A NEW LIST...
Whiny Self-Centered Jerks
AMELIA LOUISE McBRIDE
CELINE DIO
P. DIDDY
ADD TO THIS THE NAGGING QUESTION OF WHY SANTA WOULD IGNORE SOMEONE LIKE PAJAMAMAN, AND THERE WAS ONLY ONE THING I COULD DO....
TANNER? I HAVE A QUESTION.
IS THERE REALLY A SANTA CLAUS?
YA KNOW, YOU SHOULD ASK ME THESE THINGS BEFORE I HAVE THREE EGGNOGS.

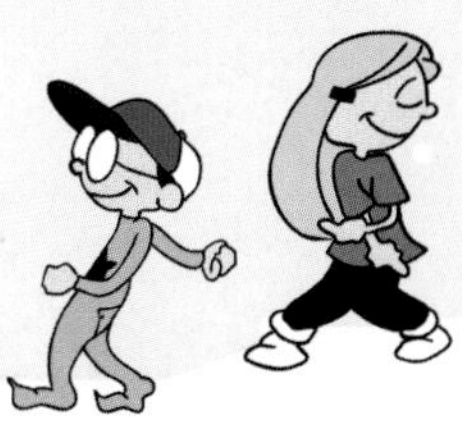

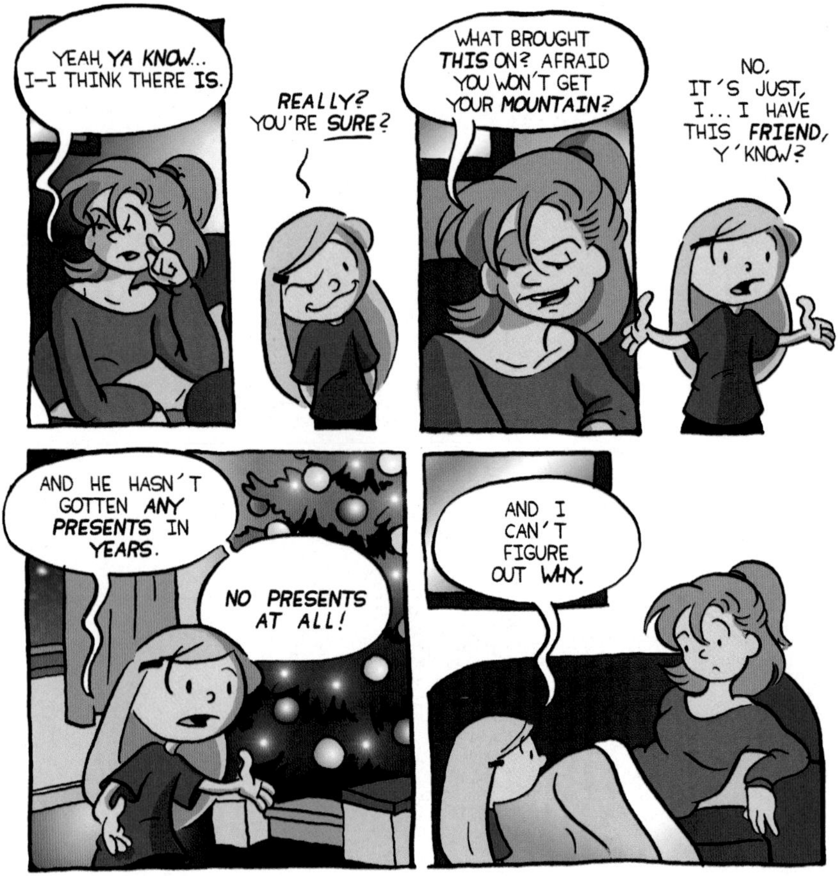
YEAH, YA KNOW... I—I THINK THERE IS.
REALLY? YOU'RE SURE?
WHAT BROUGHT THIS ON? AFRAID YOU WON'T GET YOUR MOUNTAIN?
NO. IT'S JUST, I... I HAVE THIS FRIEND, Y'KNOW?
AND HE HASN'T GOTTEN ANY PRESENTS IN YEARS.
NO PRESENTS AT ALL!
AND I CAN'T FIGURE OUT WHY.

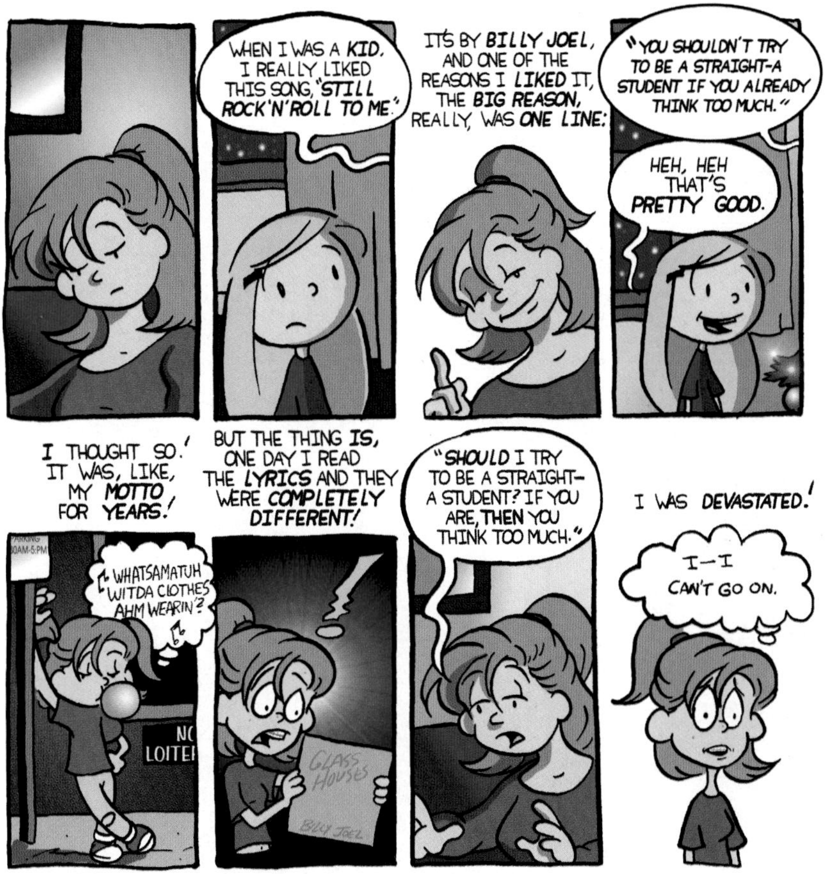
WHEN I WAS A KID, I REALLY LIKED THIS SONG, "STILL ROCK'N'ROLL TO ME."
IT'S BY BILLY JOEL, AND ONE OF THE REASONS I LIKED IT, THE BIG REASON, REALLY, WAS ONE LINE:
"YOU SHOULDN'T TRY TO BE A STRAIGHT-A STUDENT IF YOU ALREADY THINK TOO MUCH."
HEH, HEH THAT'S PRETTY GOOD.
I THOUGHT SO! IT WAS, LIKE, MY MOTTO FOR YEARS!
PARKING
WHATSAMATUH WITDA CLOTHES AHM WEARIN'?
NO LOITER
BUT THE THING IS, ONE DAY I READ THE LYRICS AND THEY WERE COMPLETELY DIFFERENT!
GLASS HOUSES
BILLY JOEL
"SHOULD I TRY TO BE A STRAIGHT-A STUDENT? IF YOU ARE, THEN YOU THINK TOO MUCH."
I WAS DEVASTATED!
I—I CAN'T GO ON.

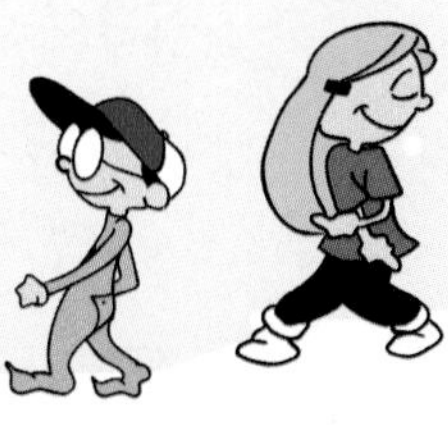

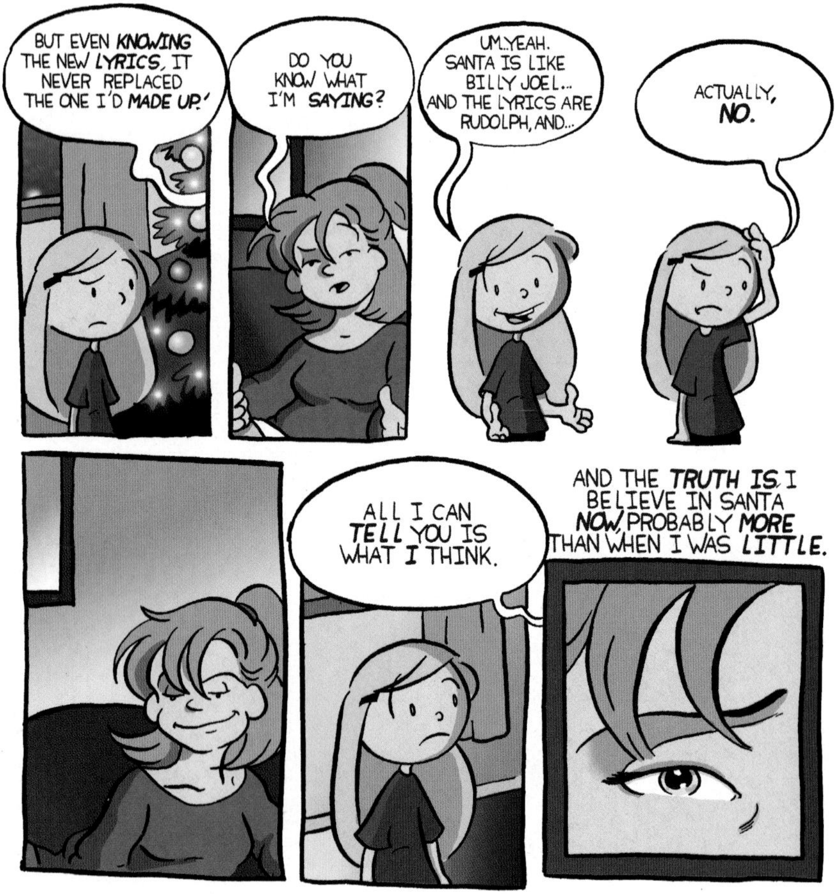
BUT EVEN KNOWING THE NEW LYRICS, IT NEVER REPLACED THE ONE I'D MADE UP.'
DO YOU KNOW WHAT I'M SAYING?
UM...YEAH. SANTA IS LIKE BILLY JOEL... AND THE LYRICS ARE RUDOLPH, AND...
ACTUALLY, NO.
ALL I CAN TELL YOU IS WHAT I THINK.
AND THE TRUTH IS, I BELIEVE IN SANTA NOW, PROBABLY MORE THAN WHEN I WAS LITTLE.

THERE IS REAL *MAGIC* AT CHRISTMAS, YA *KNOW?* I MEAN, IT'S COMPLETELY *CORNY*, AND I'D PROBABLY BE STRIPPED OF MY REPLACEMENTS *FAN CLUB MEMBERSHIP* FOR SAYING SO, BUT IT'S *TRUE*. AND ANY TIME YOU *FIND* MAGIC IN THIS WORLD, YOU HAVE TO *FIGHT HARD* TO KEEP IT.

I THINK WHAT YOU'RE *REALLY* ASKING, THOUGH, IS WHY ISN'T LIFE *FAIR*. AND I'M *SORRY*, SWEETIE, BUT I DON'T HAVE AN *ANSWER*. BUT LISTEN, YOU SHOULDN'T HAVE SUCH A *HEAVY HEART* ON CHRISTMAS EVE. SO *CLOSE YOUR EYES*, AND BE *CERTAIN* THAT SANTA IS ON HIS WAY.

AND WHEN YOU *SLEEP* DREAM OF ALL THE *GIFTS* YOU *WILL* RECEIVE.

AND THE ONES YOU *ALREADY HAVE*.

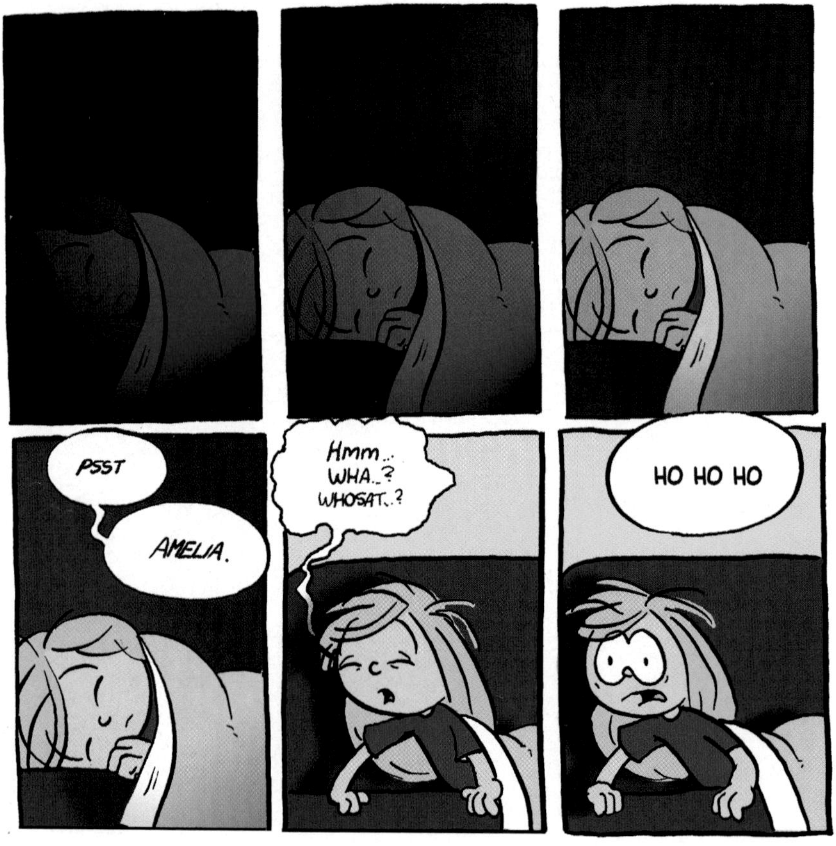
PSST
AMELIA.
Hmm..
WHA..?
WHOSAT..?
HO HO HO

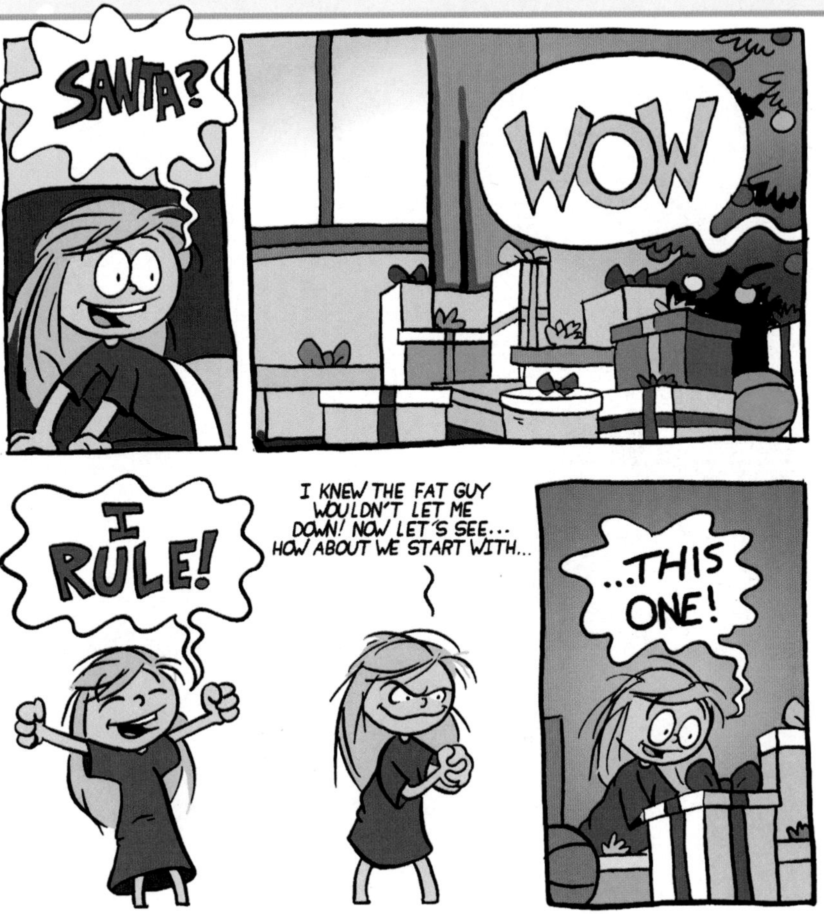
SANTA?
WOW
I RULE!
I KNEW THE FAT GUY WOULDN'T LET ME DOWN! NOW LET'S SEE... HOW ABOUT WE START WITH...
...THIS ONE!

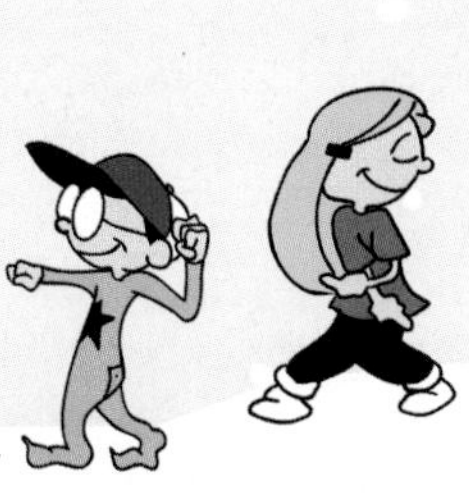

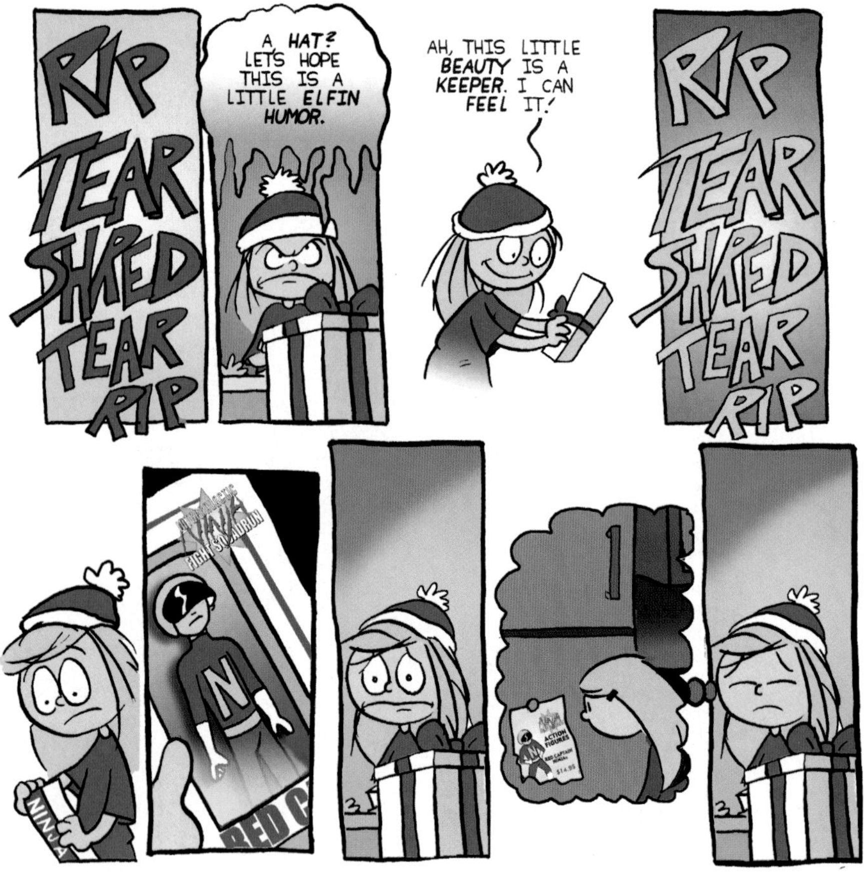
RIP
TEAR
SHRED
TEAR
RIP
A HAT? LET'S HOPE THIS IS A LITTLE ELFIN HUMOR.
AH, THIS LITTLE BEAUTY IS A KEEPER. I CAN FEEL IT!
RIP
TEAR
SHRED
TEAR
RIP
NINJA
FIGHT SQUADRON
ACTION FIGURES
RED CAPTAIN NINJA
$14.95

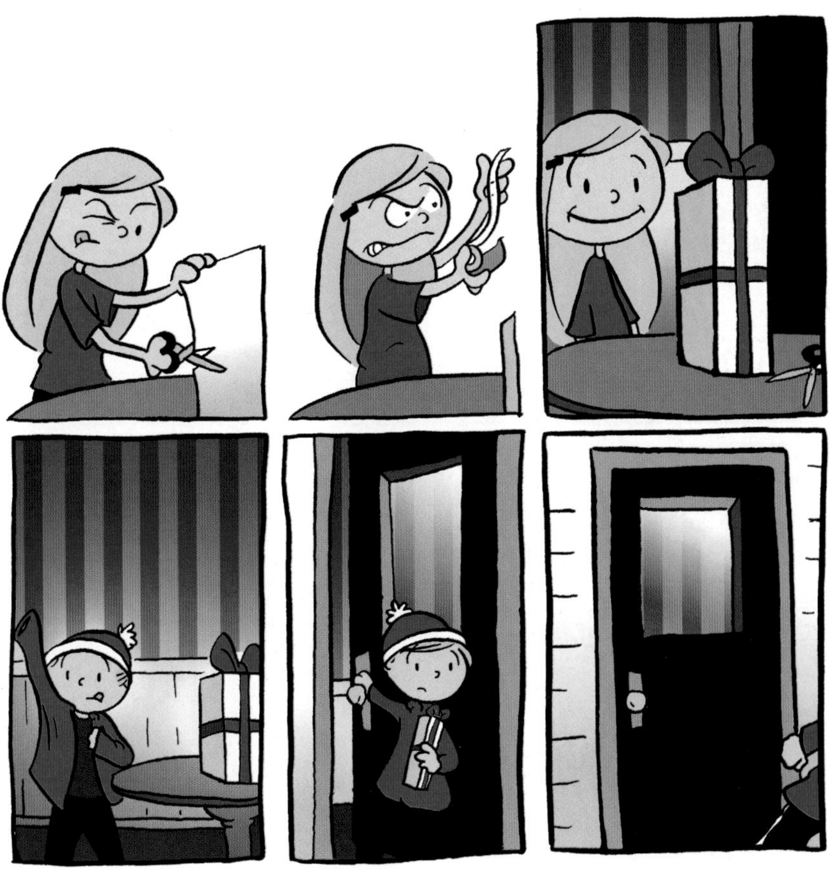

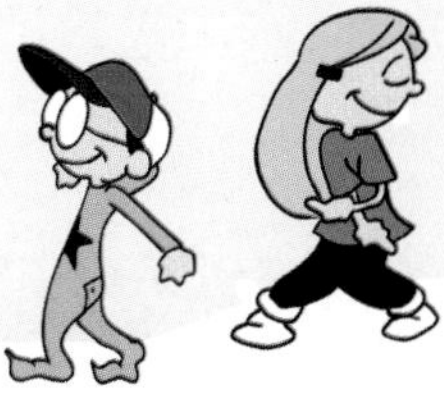

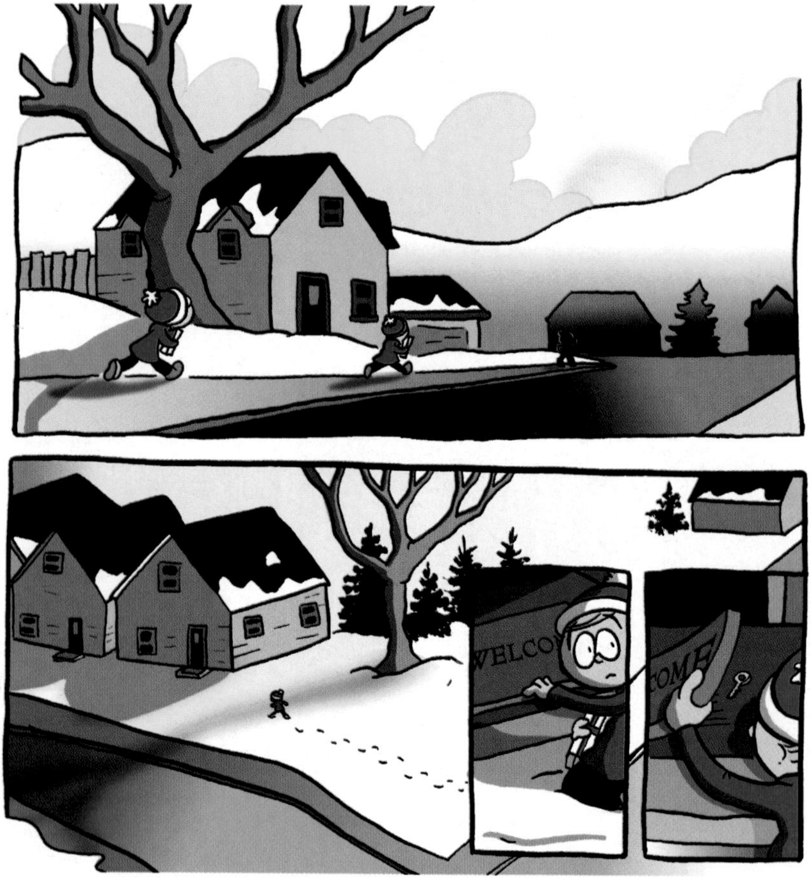

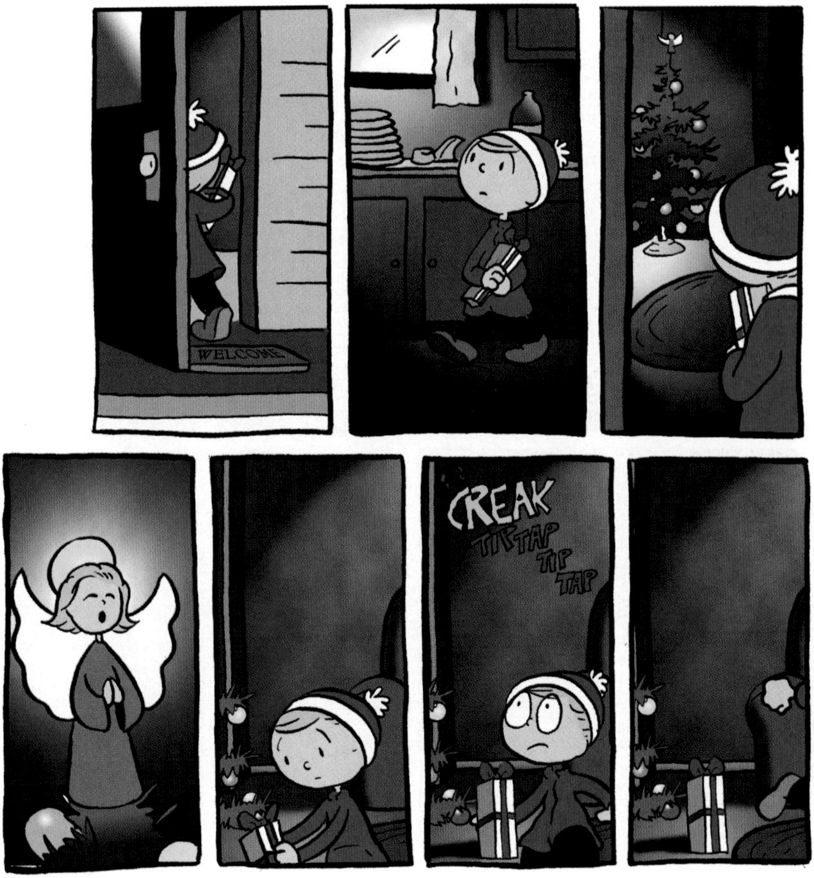
WELCOME
CREAK
TIP TAP
TIP
TAP

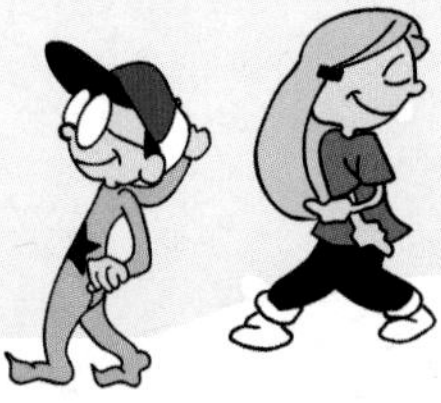

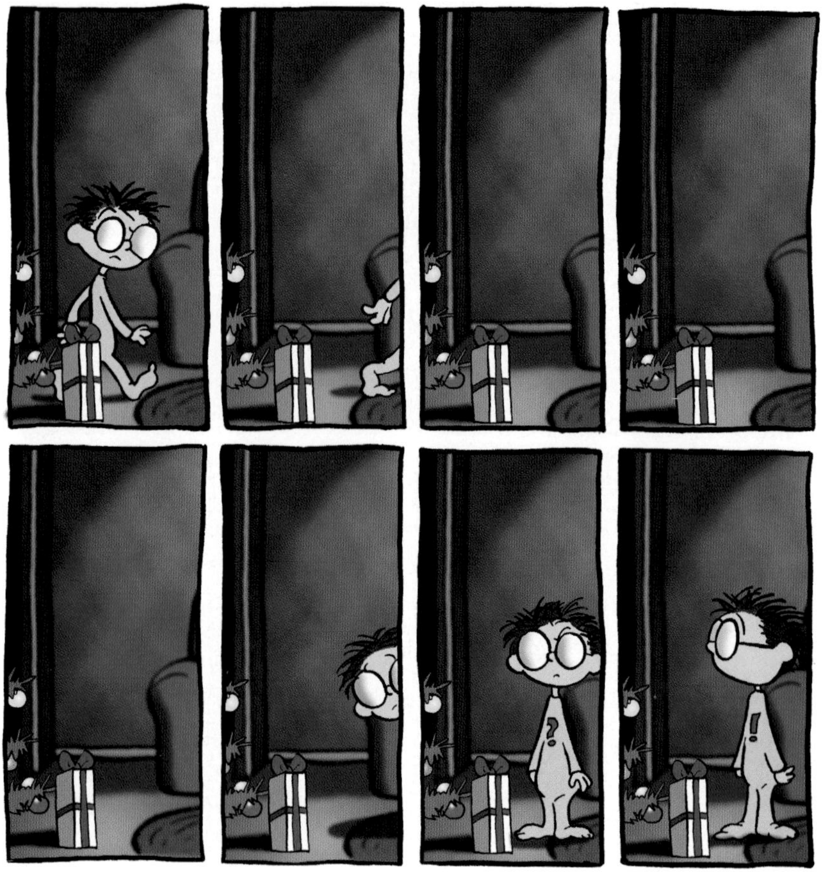

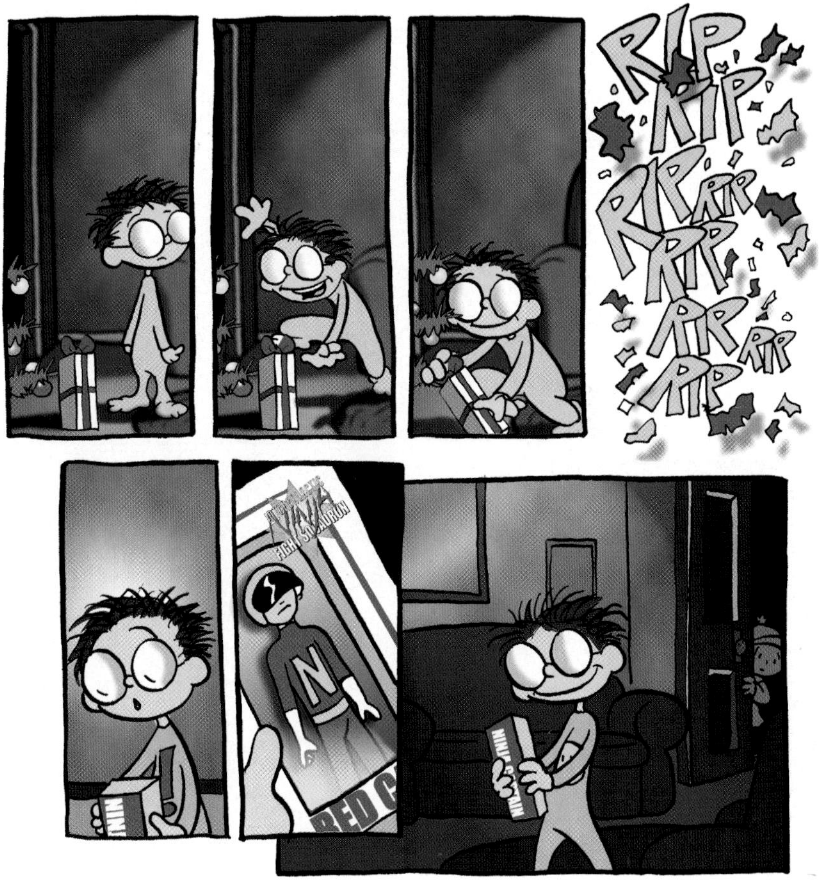
RIP
RIP
RIP
RIP
RIP
RIP
RIP
RIP
NINJA
FIGHT SQUADRON
RED C

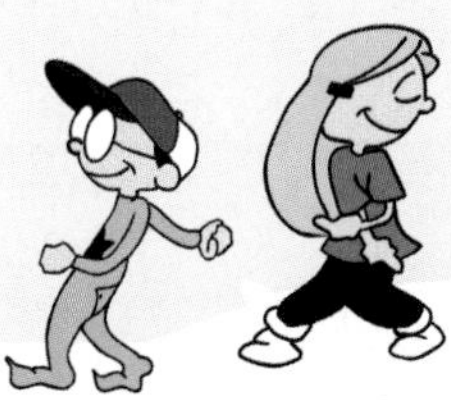

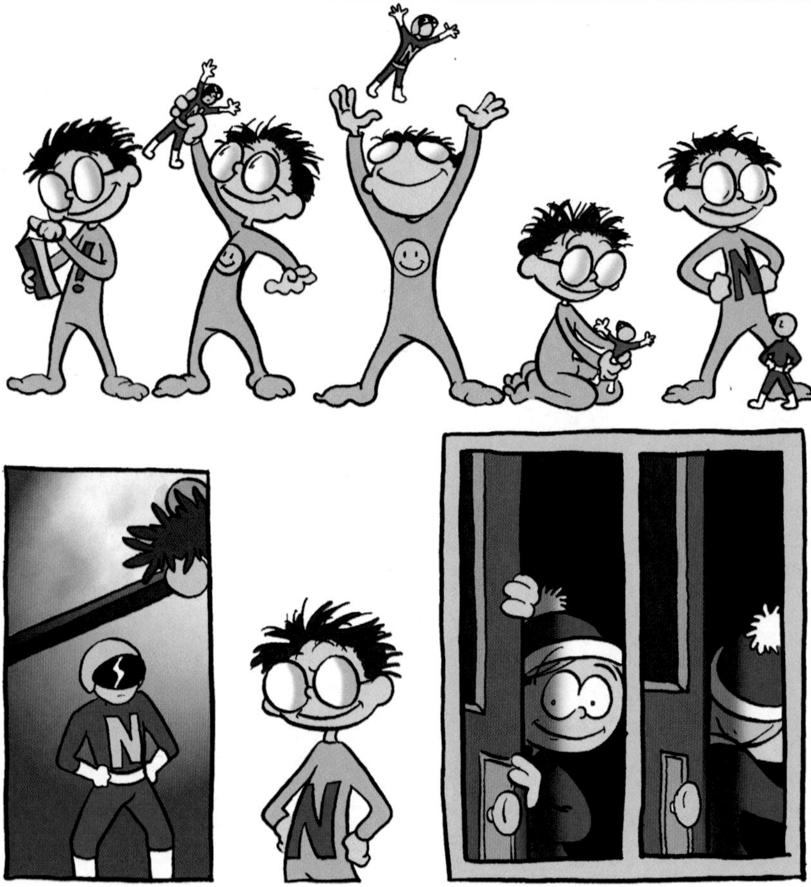

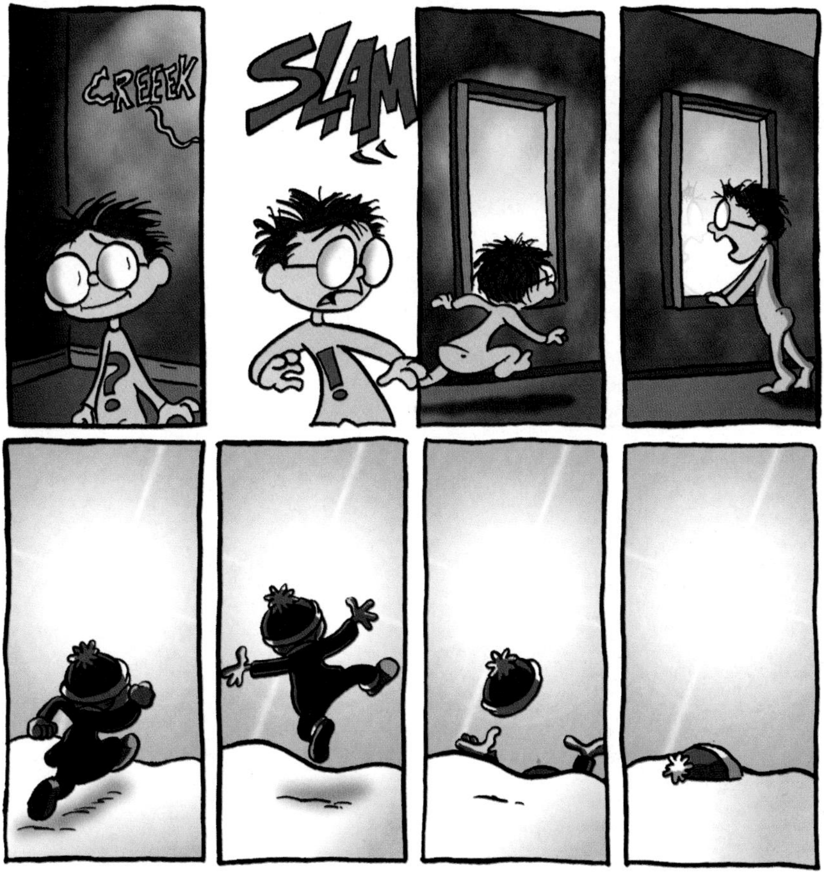
CREEEK
SLAM

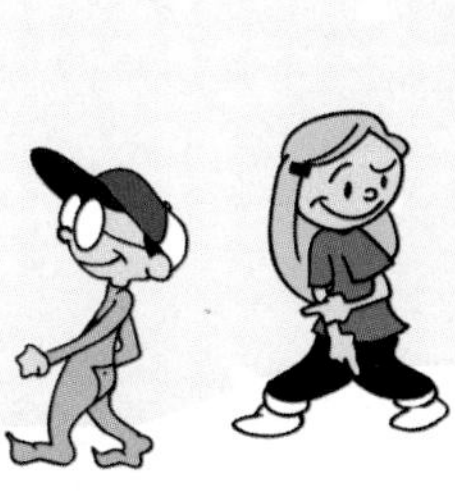

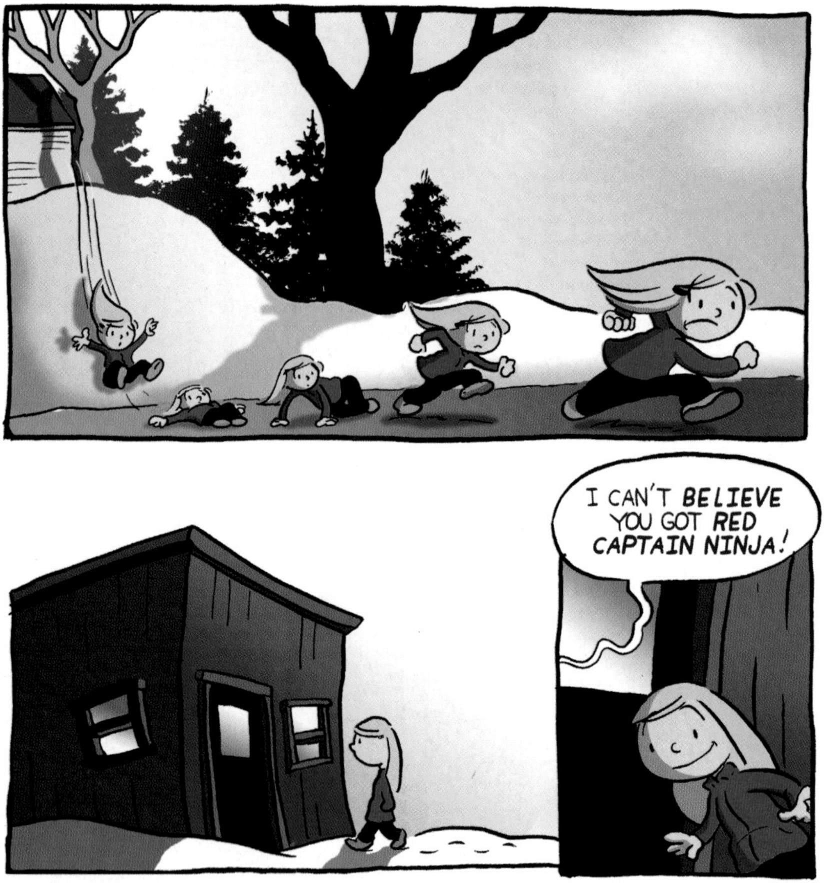
I CAN'T BELIEVE YOU GOT RED CAPTAIN NINJA!

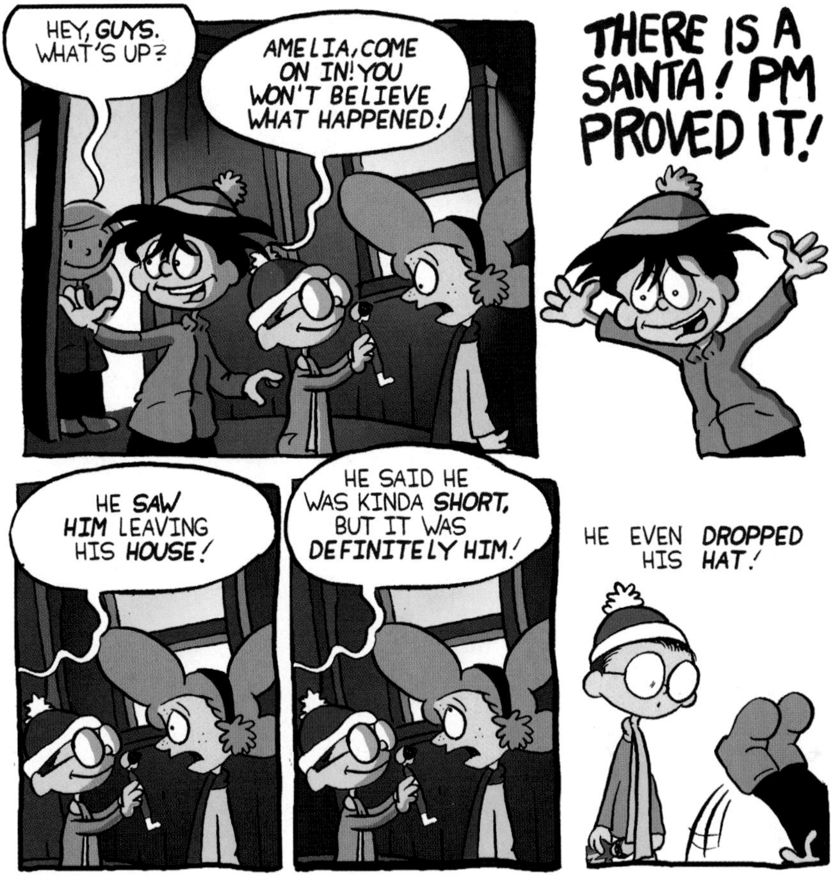
HEY, GUYS. WHAT'S UP?
AMELIA, COME ON IN! YOU WON'T BELIEVE WHAT HAPPENED!
THERE IS A SANTA! PM PROVED IT!
HE SAW HIM LEAVING HIS HOUSE!
HE SAID HE WAS KINDA SHORT, BUT IT WAS DEFINITELY HIM!
HE EVEN DROPPED HIS HAT!

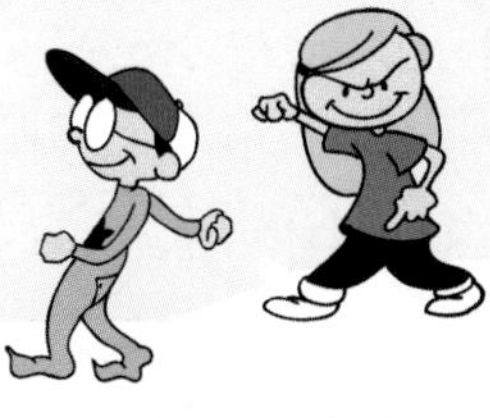

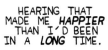

"THERE IS A SANTA."

HEARING THAT MADE ME *HAPPIER* THAN I'D BEEN IN A *LONG* TIME.

CUZ *LAST* CHRISTMAS, I LIVED WITH MY MOM *AND* DAD ON WEST 86TH STREET IN *MANHATTAN*.

NOW, I LIVE WITH MY MOM AND *HER SISTER* IN, LIKE, *NOWHERE*, PENNSYLVANIA.

AND THAT'S *FINE*. REALLY IT *IS*.

IT'S JUST THAT SOMETIMES I *MISS* THE WAY THINGS *USED* TO BE.

AND I *WISH* THAT I COULD GO *BACK*.

BUT, *REALLY*, I KNOW THAT EVEN IF I *COULD*...

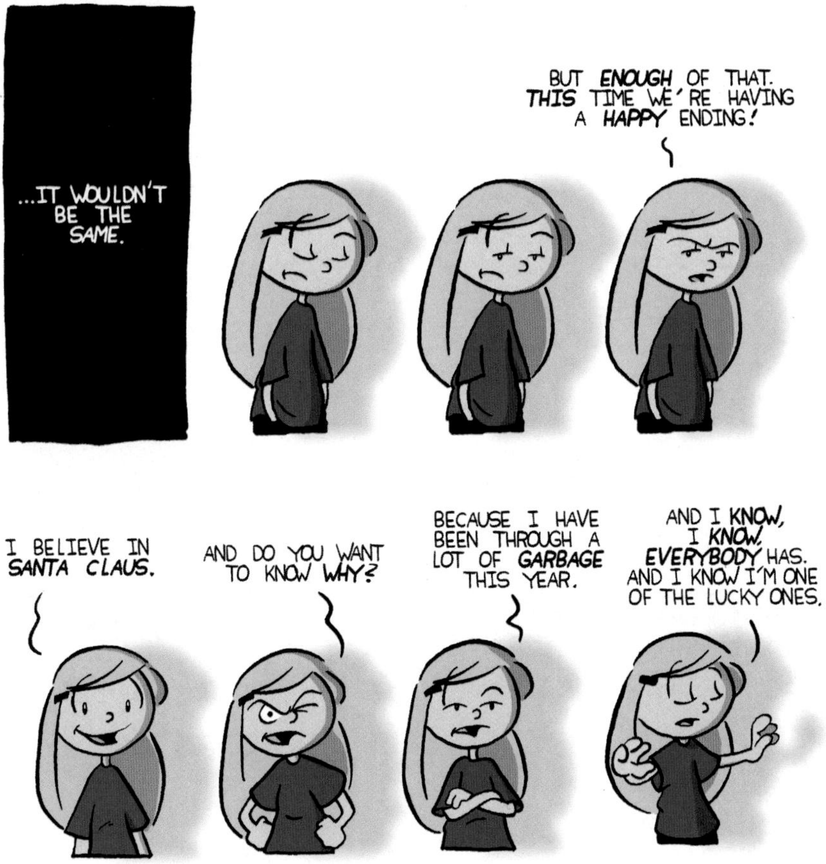
...IT WOULDN'T BE THE SAME.
BUT ENOUGH OF THAT. THIS TIME WE'RE HAVING A HAPPY ENDING!
I BELIEVE IN SANTA CLAUS.
AND DO YOU WANT TO KNOW WHY?
BECAUSE I HAVE BEEN THROUGH A LOT OF GARBAGE THIS YEAR.
AND I KNOW, I KNOW, EVERYBODY HAS. AND I KNOW I'M ONE OF THE LUCKY ONES.

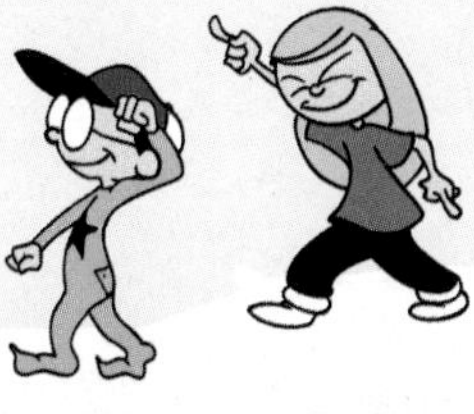

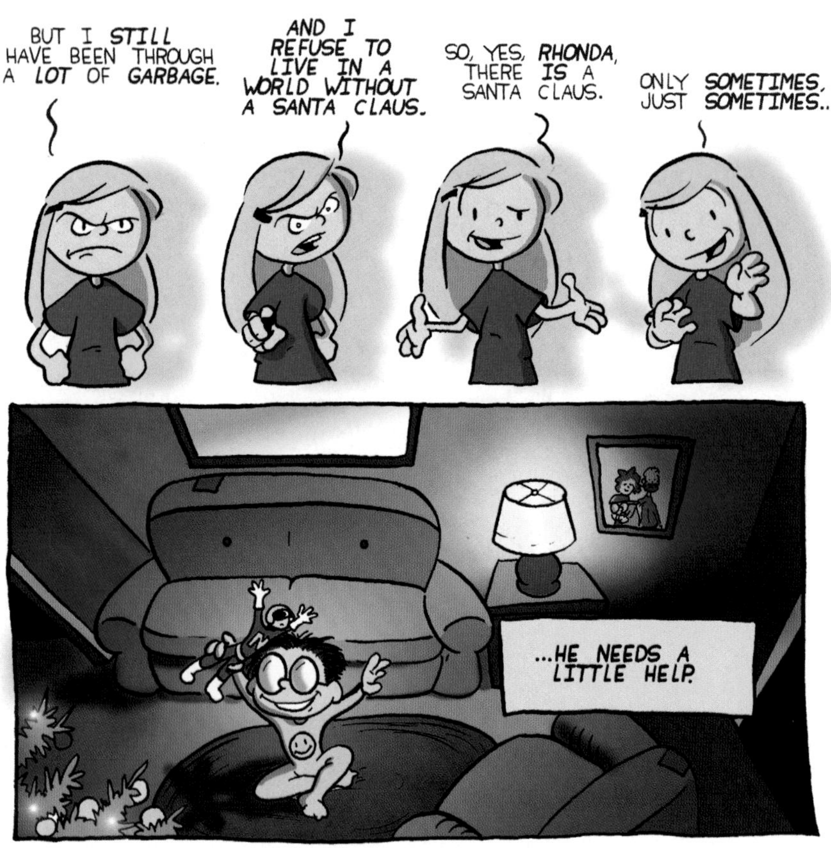
BUT I STILL HAVE BEEN THROUGH A LOT OF GARBAGE.
AND I REFUSE TO LIVE IN A WORLD WITHOUT A SANTA CLAUS.
SO, YES, RHONDA, THERE IS A SANTA CLAUS.
ONLY SOMETIMES, JUST SOMETIMES...
...HE NEEDS A LITTLE HELP.

How Amelia First Met Her Friends

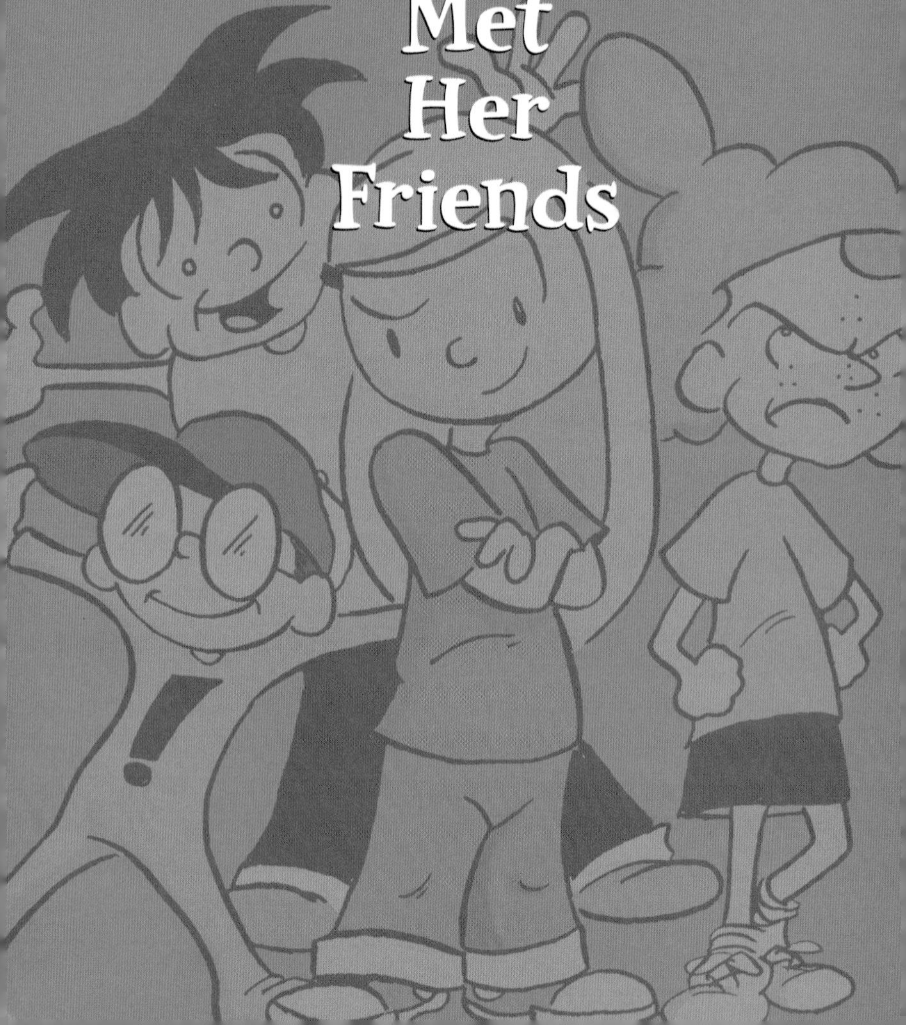

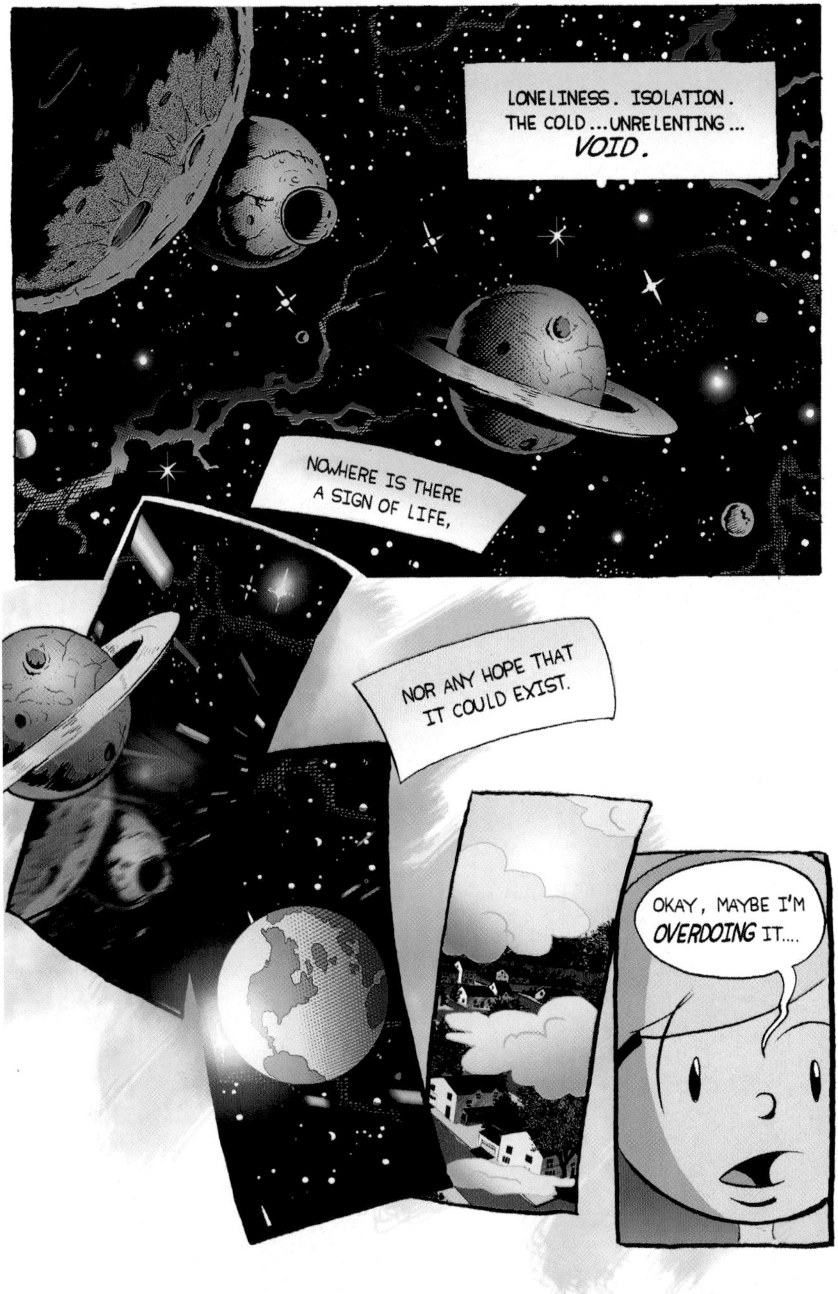
LONELINESS. ISOLATION.
THE COLD...UNRELENTING...
VOID.
NOWHERE IS THERE
A SIGN OF LIFE,
NOR ANY HOPE THAT
IT COULD EXIST.
OKAY, MAYBE I'M
OVERDOING IT....

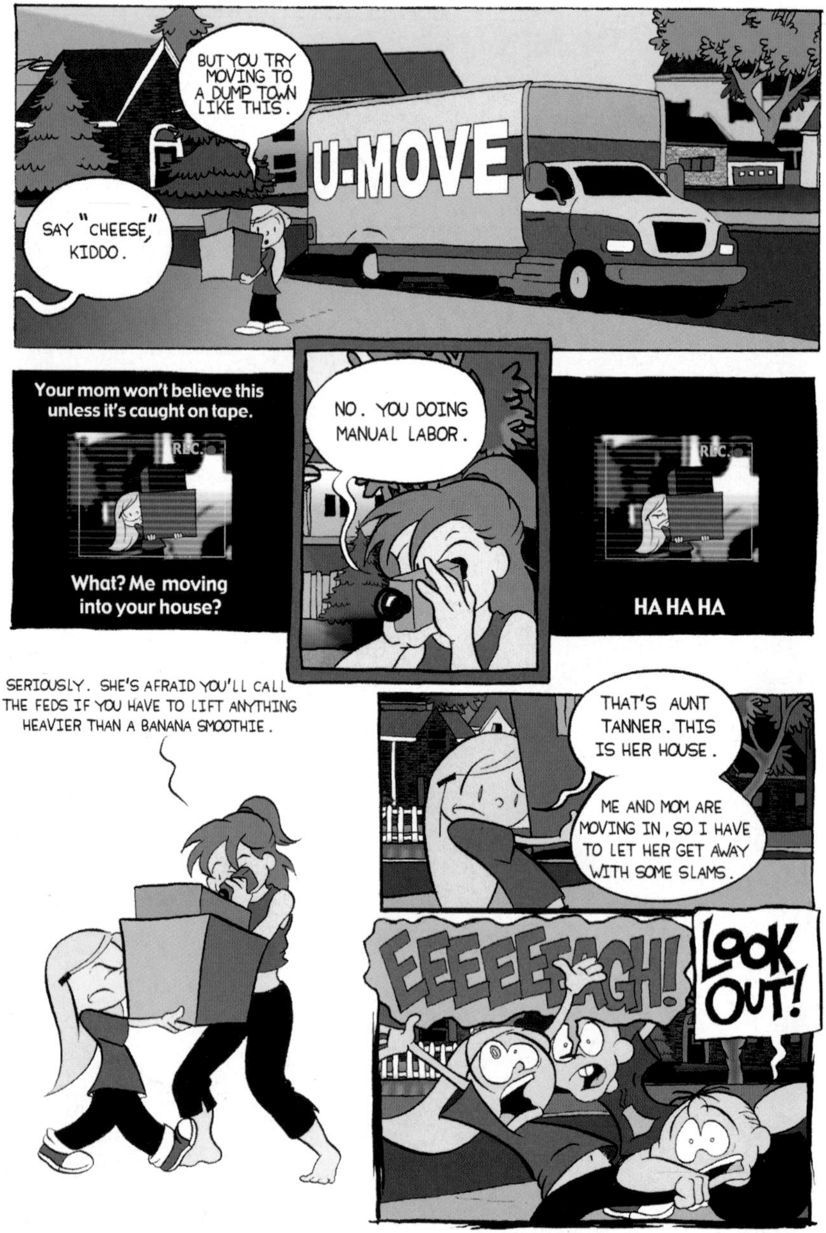
BUT YOU TRY MOVING TO A DUMP TOWN LIKE THIS.
U-MOVE
SAY "CHEESE," KIDDO.
Your mom won't believe this unless it's caught on tape.
REC.
What? Me moving into your house?
NO. YOU DOING MANUAL LABOR.
REC.
HA HA HA
SERIOUSLY. SHE'S AFRAID YOU'LL CALL THE FEDS IF YOU HAVE TO LIFT ANYTHING HEAVIER THAN A BANANA SMOOTHIE.
THAT'S AUNT TANNER. THIS IS HER HOUSE.
ME AND MOM ARE MOVING IN, SO I HAVE TO LET HER GET AWAY WITH SOME SLAMS.
EEEEEEAGH!
LOOK OUT!

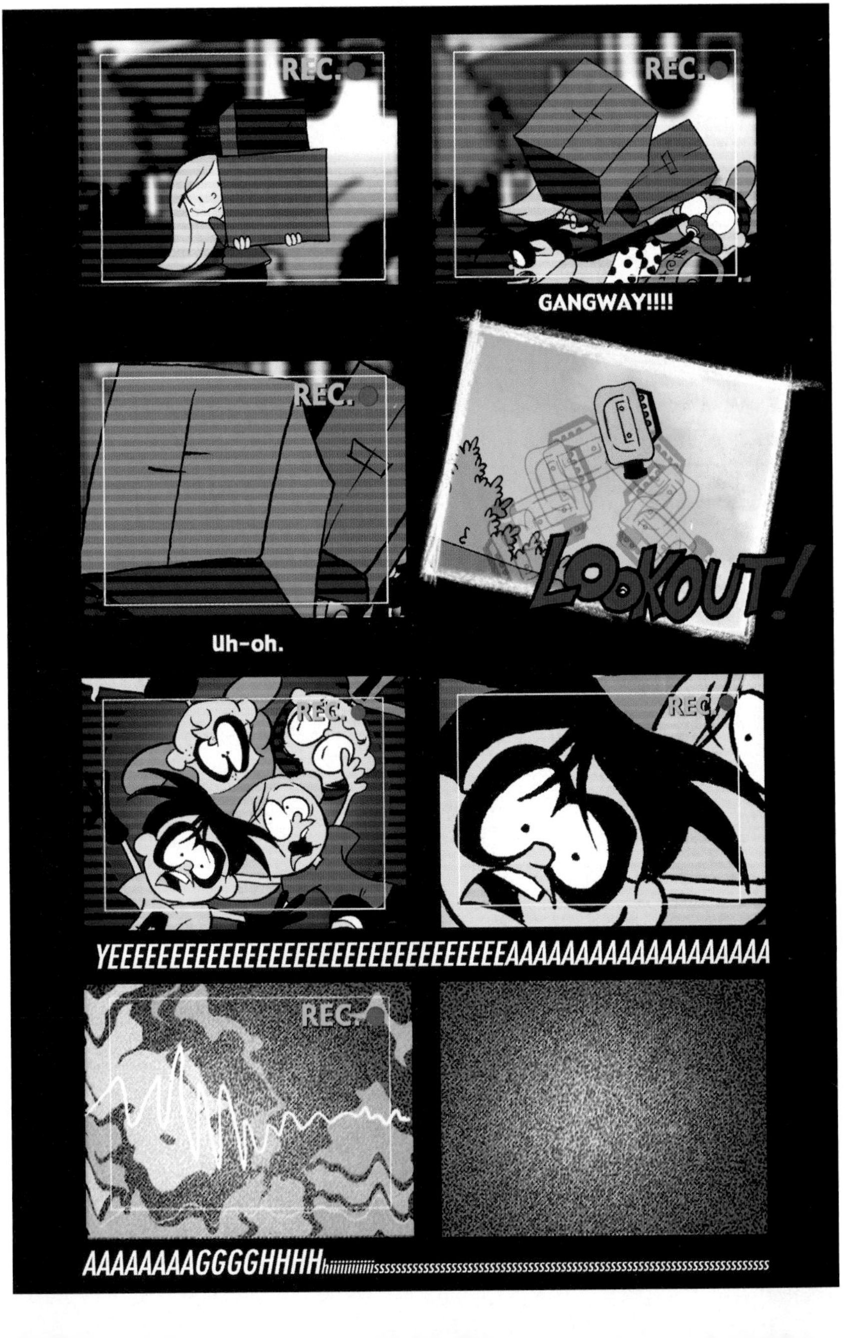
REC.
REC.
GANGWAY!!!!
REC.
Uh-oh.
LOOKOUT!
REC.
REC.
YEEEEEEEEEEEEEEEEEEEEEEEEEEEEEEAAAAAAAAAAAAAAAAA
REC.
AAAAAAAAGGGGHHHHhiiiiiiiiiiiissssssssssssssssssssssssssssssssssssssssssssssssssssssssssssssssssssssss

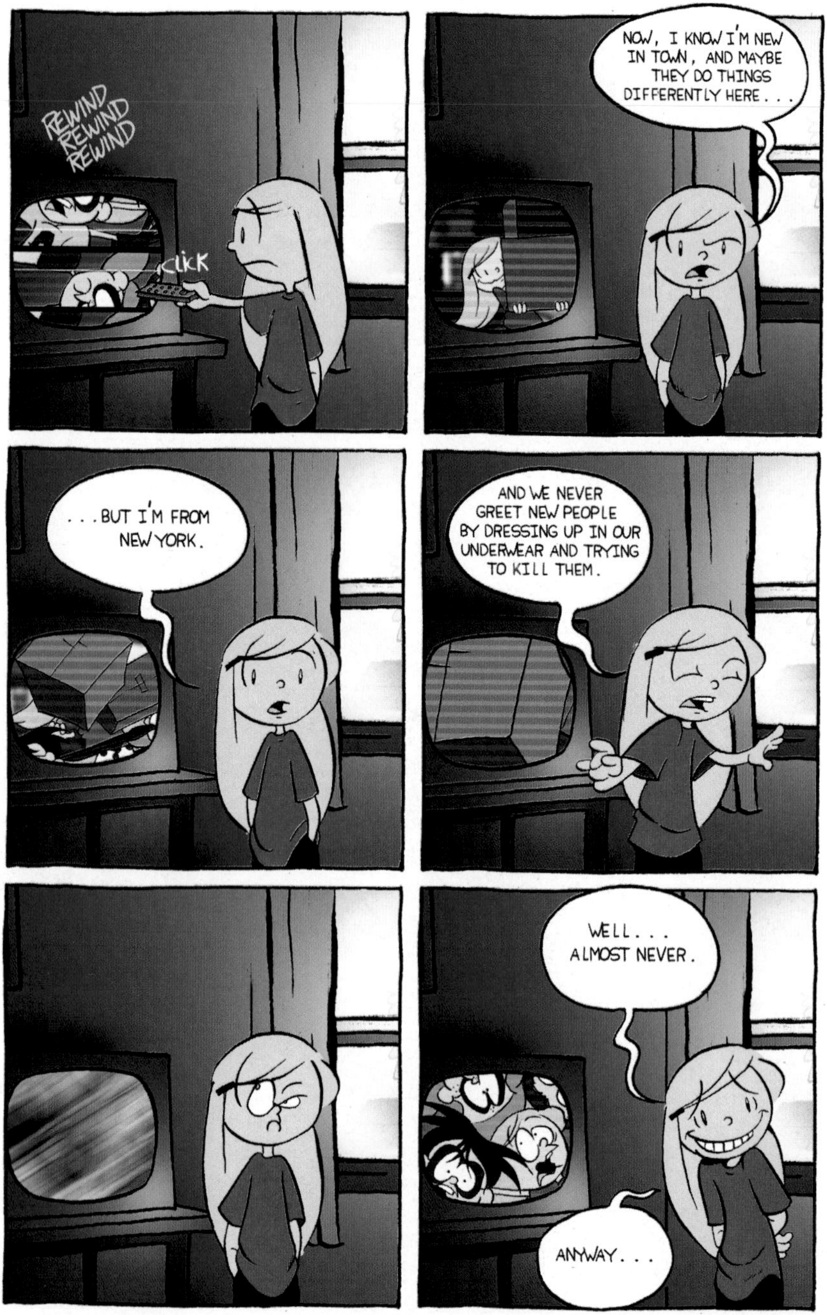
REWIND REWIND REWIND
CLICK
NOW, I KNOW I'M NEW IN TOWN, AND MAYBE THEY DO THINGS DIFFERENTLY HERE . . .
. . . BUT I'M FROM NEW YORK.
AND WE NEVER GREET NEW PEOPLE BY DRESSING UP IN OUR UNDERWEAR AND TRYING TO KILL THEM.
WELL . . . ALMOST NEVER.
ANYWAY . . .

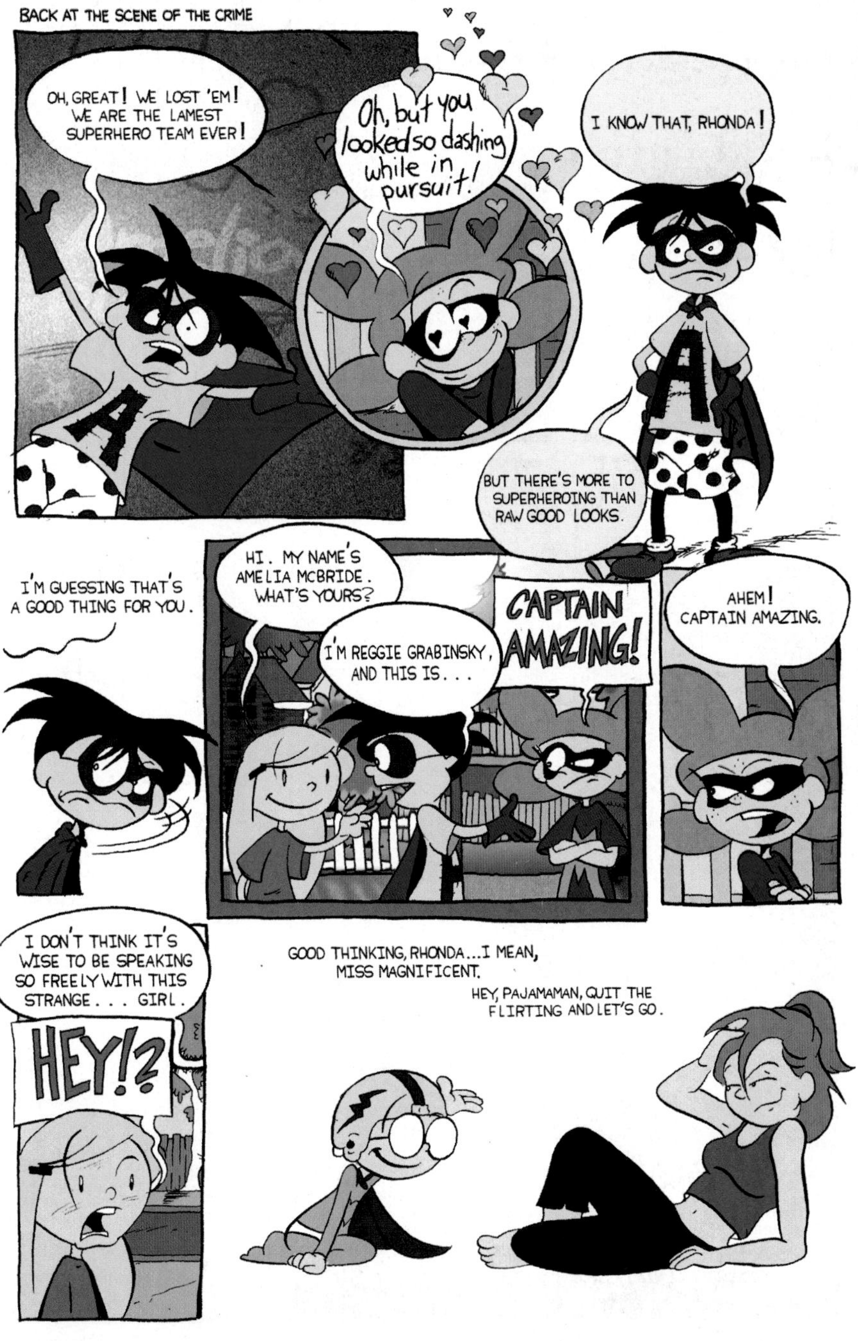
BACK AT THE SCENE OF THE CRIME
OH, GREAT! WE LOST 'EM! WE ARE THE LAMEST SUPERHERO TEAM EVER!
Oh, but you looked so dashing while in pursuit!
I KNOW THAT, RHONDA!
BUT THERE'S MORE TO SUPERHEROING THAN RAW GOOD LOOKS.
I'M GUESSING THAT'S A GOOD THING FOR YOU.
HI. MY NAME'S AMELIA MCBRIDE. WHAT'S YOURS?
I'M REGGIE GRABINSKY, AND THIS IS . . .
CAPTAIN AMAZING!
AHEM! CAPTAIN AMAZING.
I DON'T THINK IT'S WISE TO BE SPEAKING SO FREELY WITH THIS STRANGE . . . GIRL.
HEY!?
GOOD THINKING, RHONDA...I MEAN, MISS MAGNIFICENT.
HEY, PAJAMAMAN, QUIT THE FLIRTING AND LET'S GO.

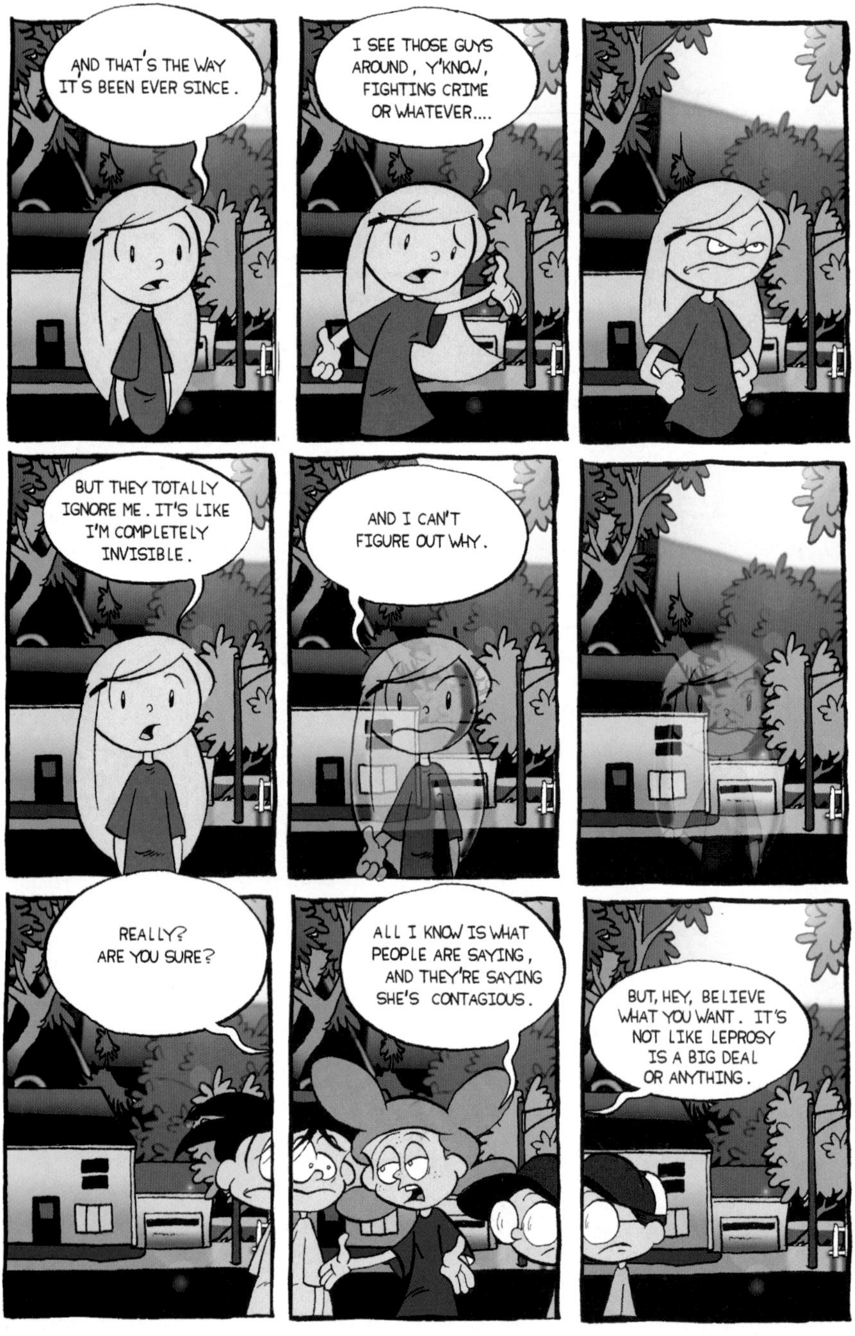
AND THAT'S THE WAY IT'S BEEN EVER SINCE.
I SEE THOSE GUYS AROUND, Y'KNOW, FIGHTING CRIME OR WHATEVER....
BUT THEY TOTALLY IGNORE ME. IT'S LIKE I'M COMPLETELY INVISIBLE.
AND I CAN'T FIGURE OUT WHY.
REALLY? ARE YOU SURE?
ALL I KNOW IS WHAT PEOPLE ARE SAYING, AND THEY'RE SAYING SHE'S CONTAGIOUS.
BUT, HEY, BELIEVE WHAT YOU WANT. IT'S NOT LIKE LEPROSY IS A BIG DEAL OR ANYTHING.

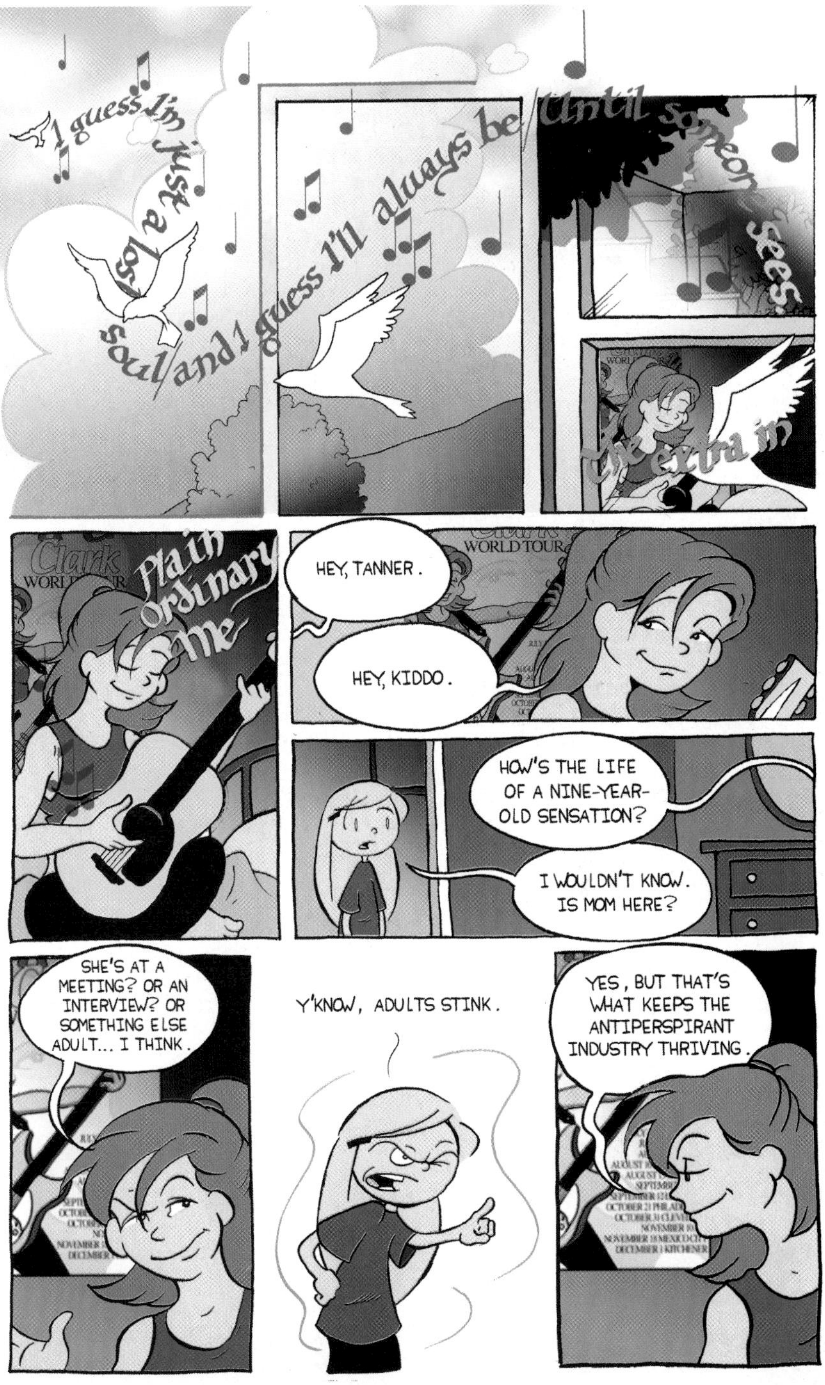

I guess I'm just a lost soul/and I guess I'll always be/Until someone sees
the extra in
Plain Ordinary Me
Clark WORLD TOUR
HEY, TANNER.
HEY, KIDDO.
HOW'S THE LIFE OF A NINE-YEAR-OLD SENSATION?
I WOULDN'T KNOW. IS MOM HERE?
SHE'S AT A MEETING? OR AN INTERVIEW? OR SOMETHING ELSE ADULT... I THINK.
Y'KNOW, ADULTS STINK.
YES, BUT THAT'S WHAT KEEPS THE ANTIPERSPIRANT INDUSTRY THRIVING.

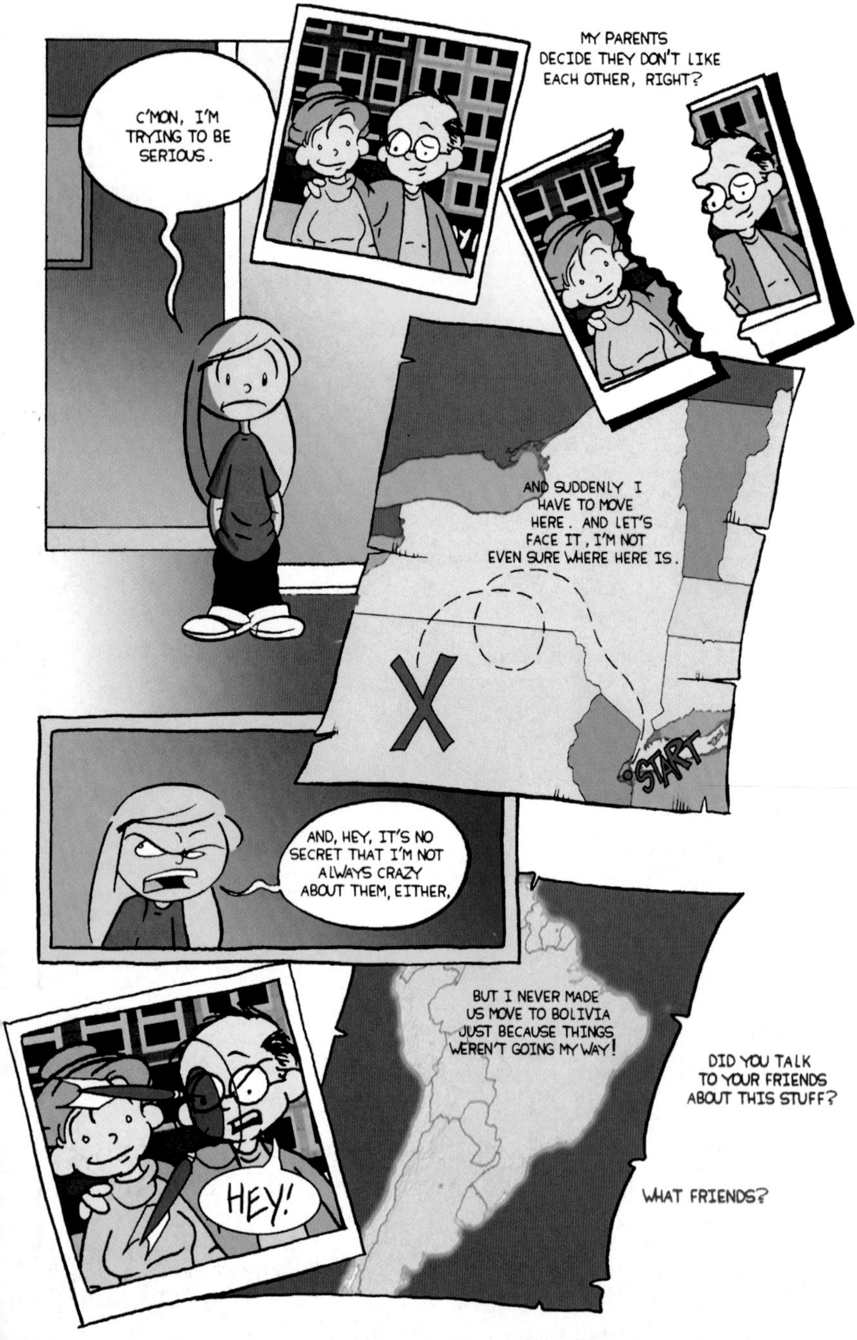
C'MON, I'M TRYING TO BE SERIOUS.
MY PARENTS DECIDE THEY DON'T LIKE EACH OTHER, RIGHT?
AND SUDDENLY I HAVE TO MOVE HERE. AND LET'S FACE IT, I'M NOT EVEN SURE WHERE HERE IS.
X
START
AND, HEY, IT'S NO SECRET THAT I'M NOT ALWAYS CRAZY ABOUT THEM, EITHER,
BUT I NEVER MADE US MOVE TO BOLIVIA JUST BECAUSE THINGS WEREN'T GOING MY WAY!
HEY!
DID YOU TALK TO YOUR FRIENDS ABOUT THIS STUFF?
WHAT FRIENDS?

OH.

Y'KNOW WHAT?

WHAT?

IT'S ALWAYS HARD WHEN YOU'RE IN A NEW PLACE...

...BUT EVERYTHING WILL WORK OUT.

YOU'RE A SPECIAL KID. THEY'LL NOTICE EVENTUALLY. THEY ALWAYS DO.

REALLY? THEY DO?

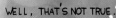

WELL, THAT'S NOT TRUE.

THEY DON'T ALWAYS NOTICE.

SOME OF THE MOST SPECIAL PEOPLE IN THE WORLD SEEM NEVER TO BE NOTICED.

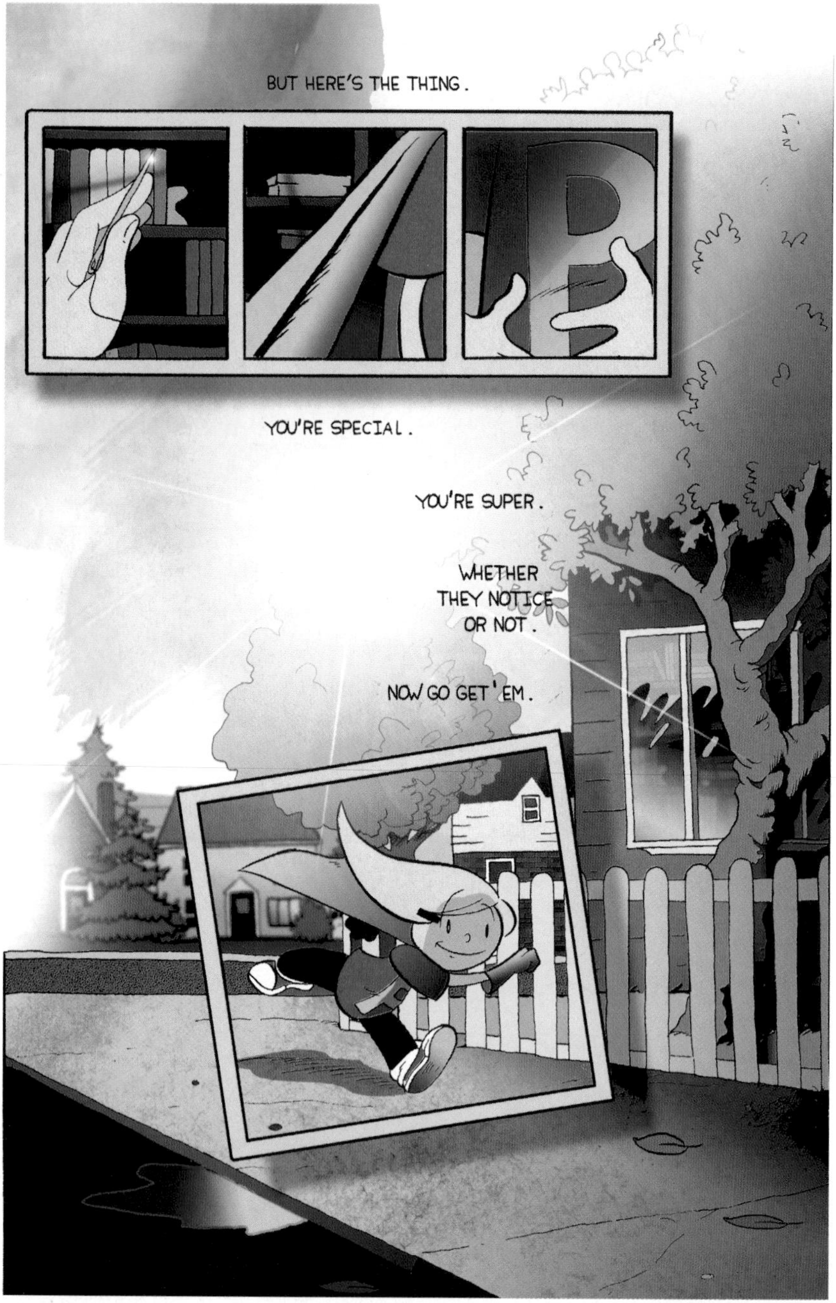
BUT HERE'S THE THING.
YOU'RE SPECIAL.
YOU'RE SUPER.
WHETHER THEY NOTICE OR NOT.
NOW GO GET 'EM.

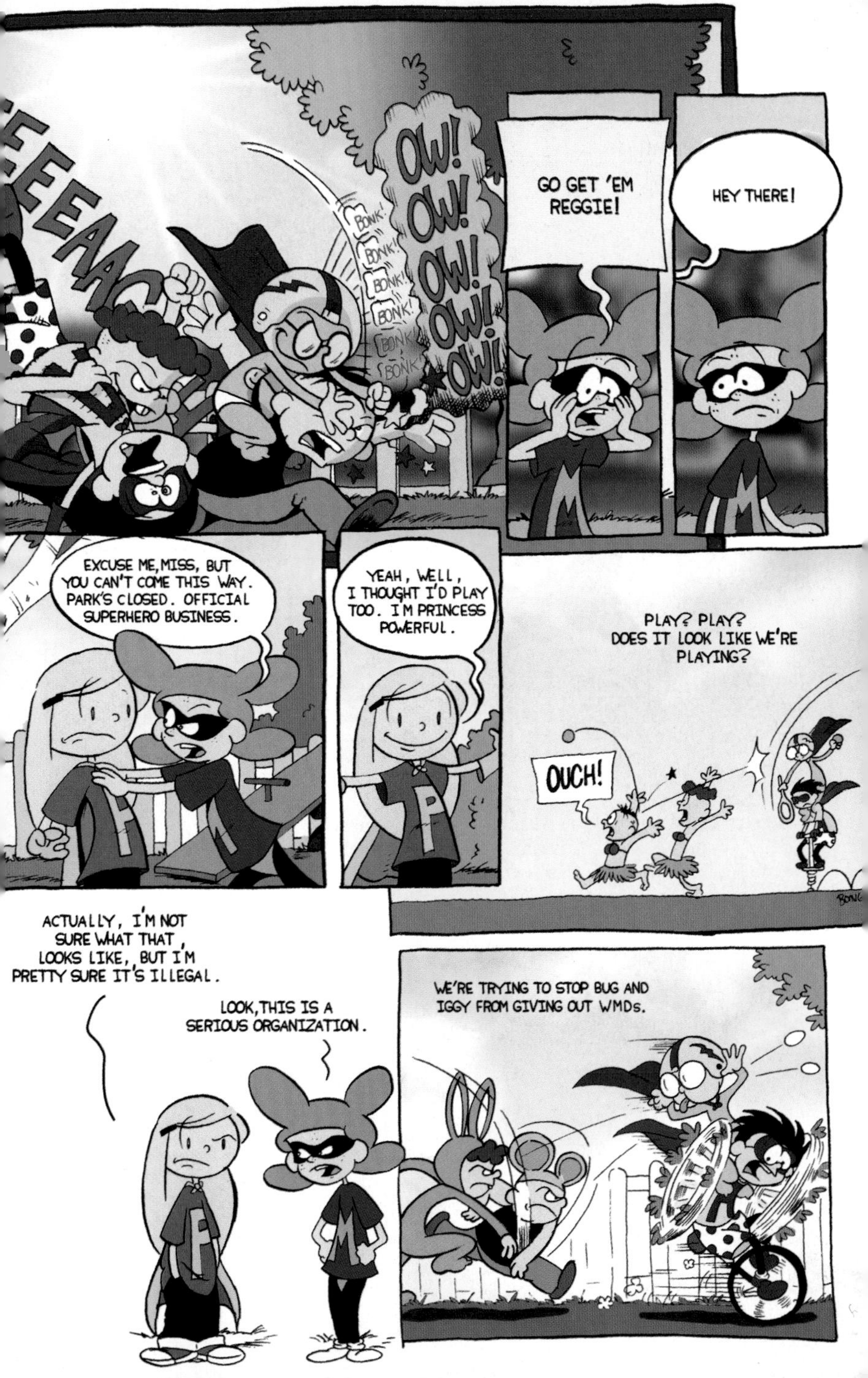
EEEAAAG
BONK! BONK! BONK! BONK! BONK! BONK!
OW! OW! OW! OW! OW!
GO GET 'EM REGGIE!
HEY THERE!
EXCUSE ME, MISS, BUT YOU CAN'T COME THIS WAY. PARK'S CLOSED. OFFICIAL SUPERHERO BUSINESS.
YEAH, WELL, I THOUGHT I'D PLAY TOO. I'M PRINCESS POWERFUL.
PLAY? PLAY? DOES IT LOOK LIKE WE'RE PLAYING?
OUCH!
BONG
ACTUALLY, I'M NOT SURE WHAT THAT LOOKS LIKE, BUT I'M PRETTY SURE IT'S ILLEGAL.
LOOK, THIS IS A SERIOUS ORGANIZATION.
WE'RE TRYING TO STOP BUG AND IGGY FROM GIVING OUT WMDs.

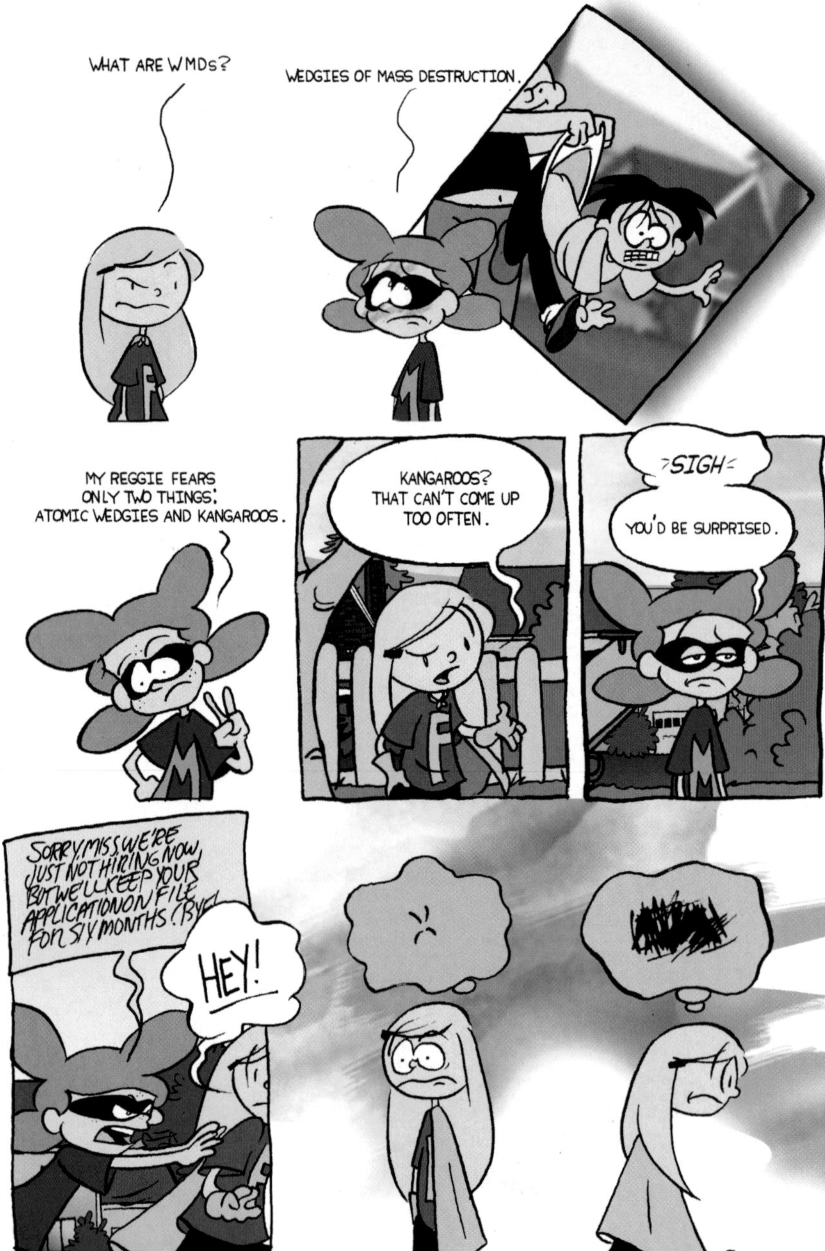
WHAT ARE WMDs?
WEDGIES OF MASS DESTRUCTION.
MY REGGIE FEARS ONLY TWO THINGS: ATOMIC WEDGIES AND KANGAROOS.
KANGAROOS? THAT CAN'T COME UP TOO OFTEN.
SIGH
YOU'D BE SURPRISED.
SORRY, MISS, WE'RE JUST NOT HIRING NOW, BUT WE'LL KEEP YOUR APPLICATION ON FILE FOR SIX MONTHS! BYE!
HEY!

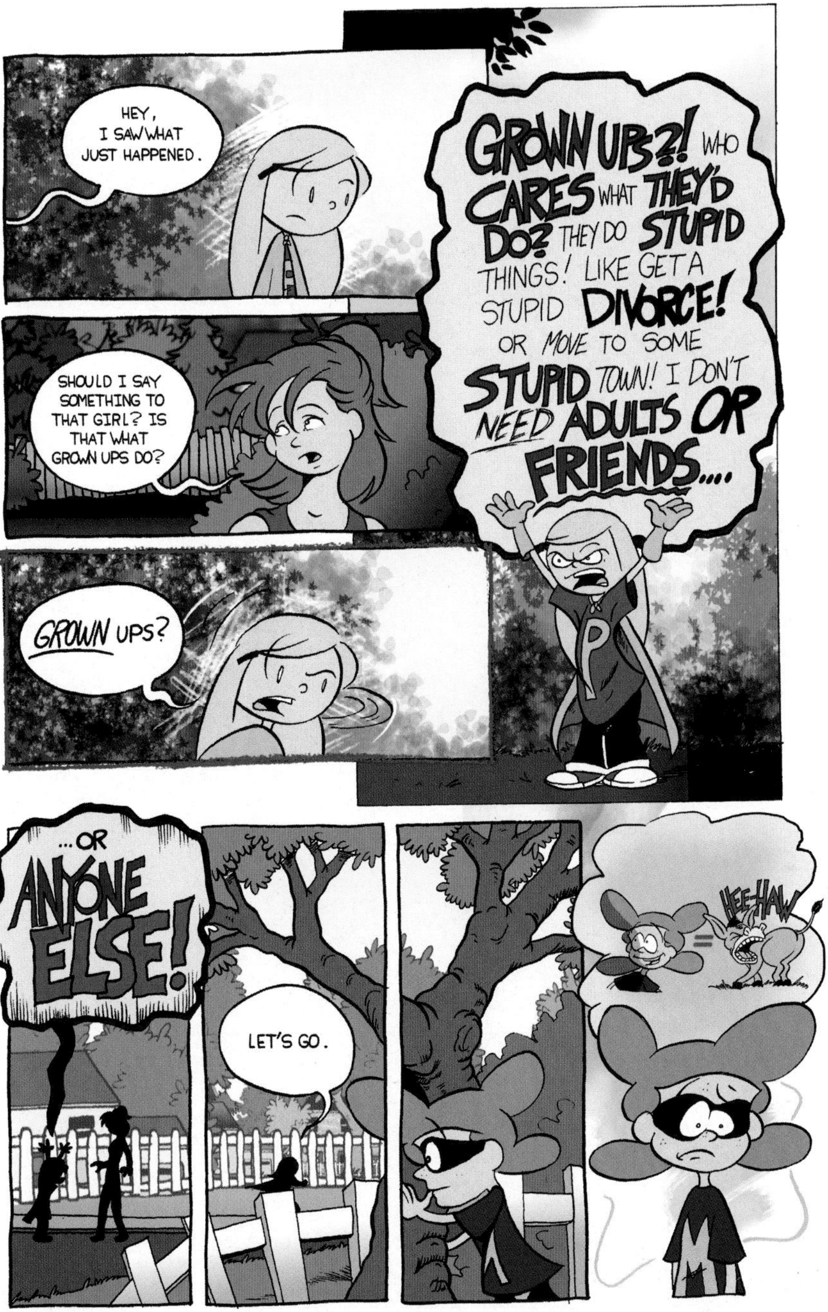
HEY, I SAW WHAT JUST HAPPENED.
SHOULD I SAY SOMETHING TO THAT GIRL? IS THAT WHAT GROWN UPS DO?
GROWN UPS?
GROWN UPS?! WHO CARES WHAT THEY'D DO? THEY DO STUPID THINGS! LIKE GET A STUPID DIVORCE! OR MOVE TO SOME STUPID TOWN! I DON'T NEED ADULTS OR FRIENDS....
...OR ANYONE ELSE!
LET'S GO.
HEE-HAW

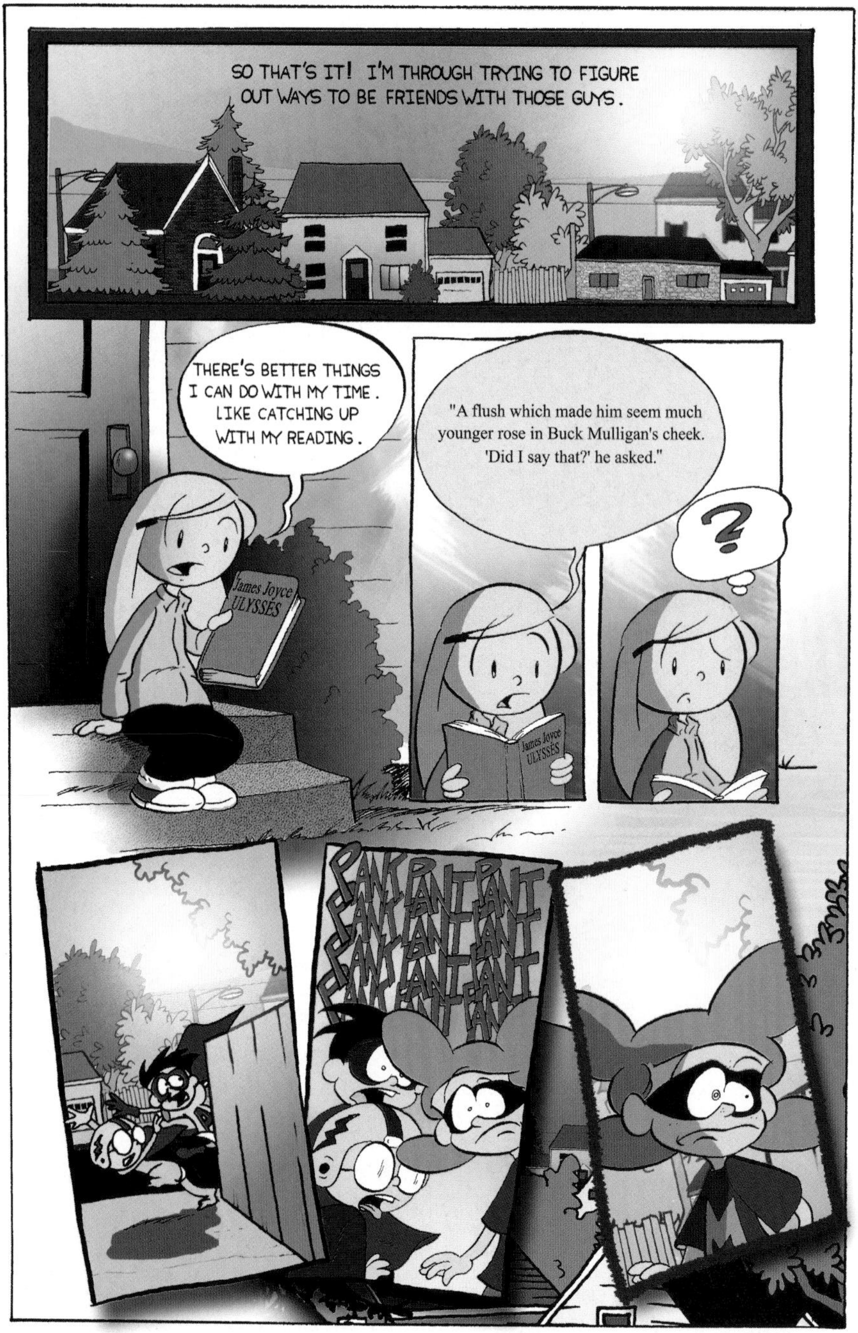
SO THAT'S IT! I'M THROUGH TRYING TO FIGURE OUT WAYS TO BE FRIENDS WITH THOSE GUYS.
THERE'S BETTER THINGS I CAN DO WITH MY TIME. LIKE CATCHING UP WITH MY READING.
James Joyce ULYSSES
"A flush which made him seem much younger rose in Buck Mulligan's cheek. 'Did I say that?' he asked."
James Joyce ULYSSES
?

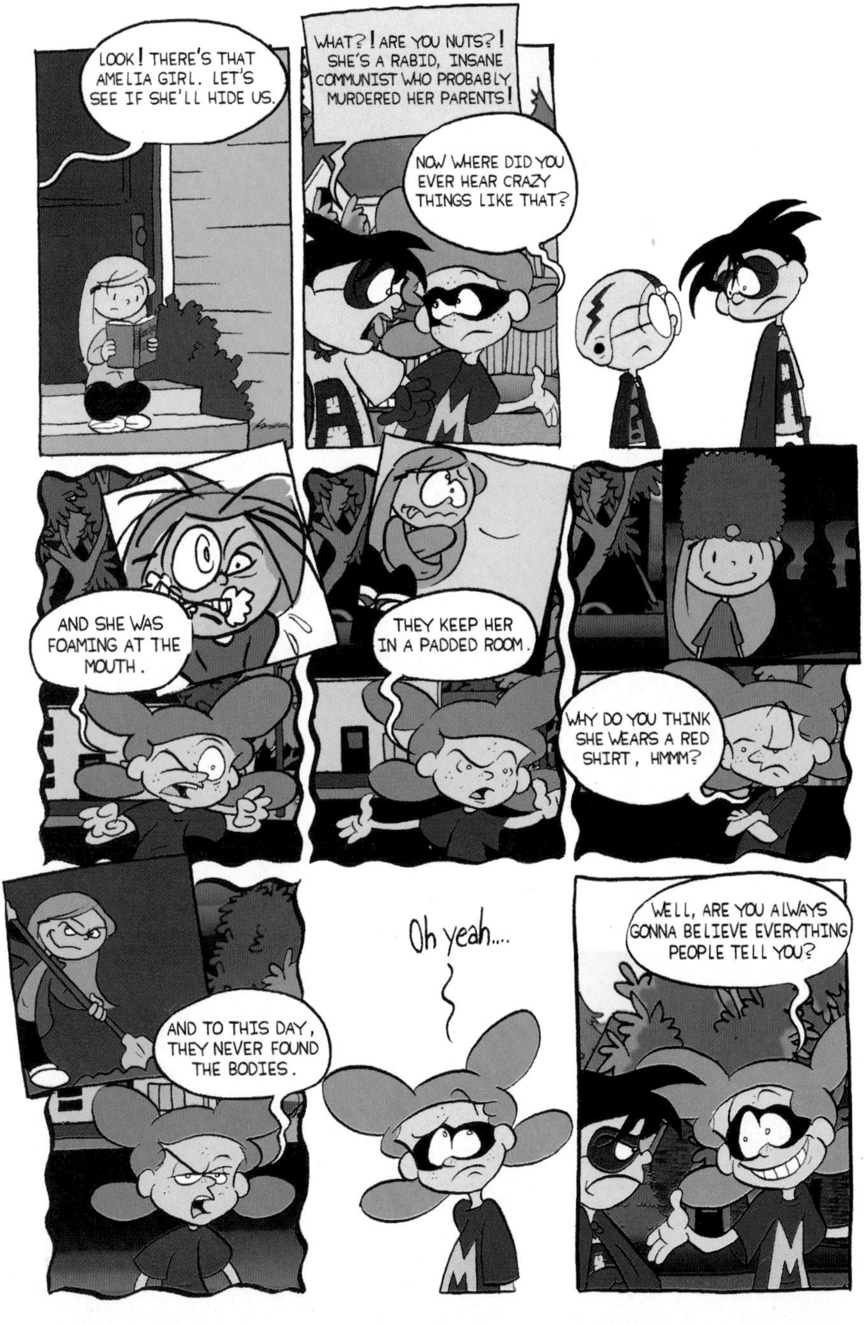
LOOK! THERE'S THAT AMELIA GIRL. LET'S SEE IF SHE'LL HIDE US.
WHAT?! ARE YOU NUTS?! SHE'S A RABID, INSANE COMMUNIST WHO PROBABLY MURDERED HER PARENTS!
NOW WHERE DID YOU EVER HEAR CRAZY THINGS LIKE THAT?
AND SHE WAS FOAMING AT THE MOUTH.
THEY KEEP HER IN A PADDED ROOM.
WHY DO YOU THINK SHE WEARS A RED SHIRT, HMMM?
AND TO THIS DAY, THEY NEVER FOUND THE BODIES.
Oh yeah....
WELL, ARE YOU ALWAYS GONNA BELIEVE EVERYTHING PEOPLE TELL YOU?

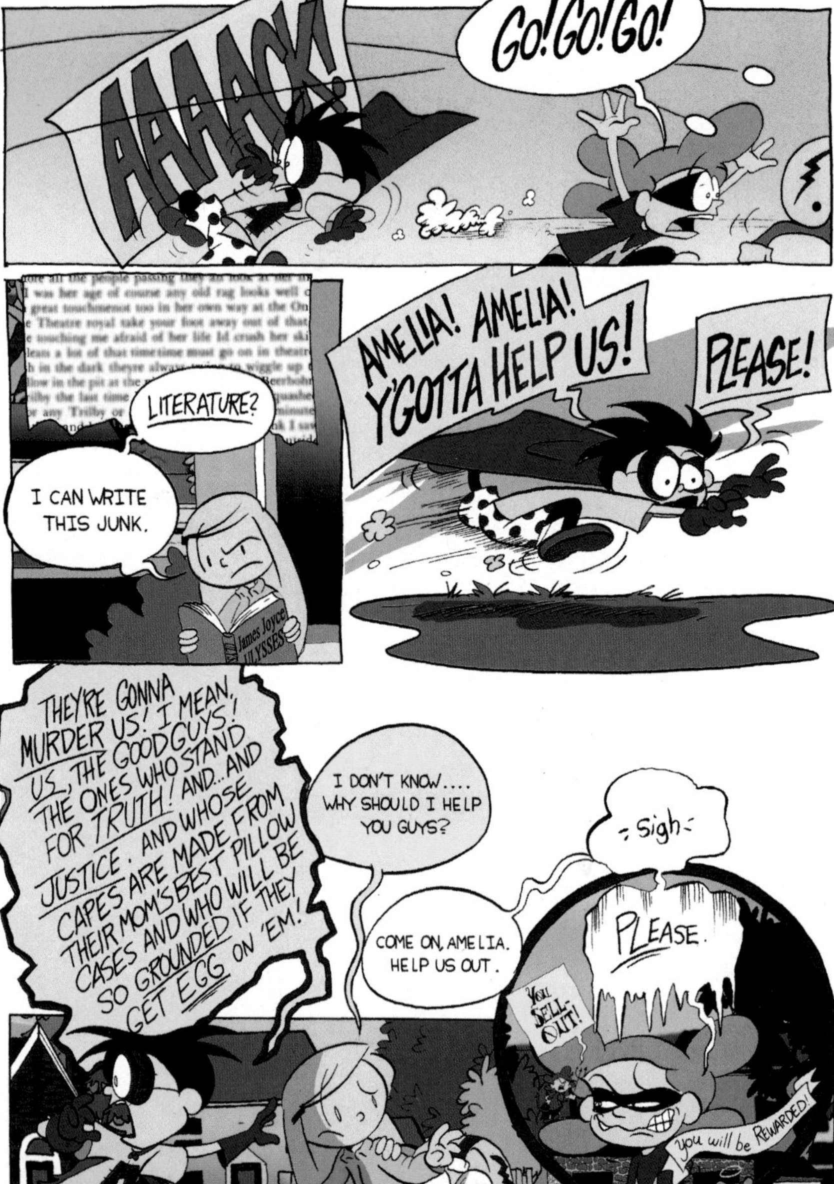
AAAACK!
GO! GO! GO!
LITERATURE?
I CAN WRITE THIS JUNK.
James Joyce ULYSSES
AMELIA! AMELIA! Y'GOTTA HELP US!
PLEASE!
THEY'RE GONNA MURDER US! I MEAN, US, THE GOOD GUYS! THE ONES WHO STAND FOR TRUTH! AND... AND JUSTICE. AND WHOSE CAPES ARE MADE FROM THEIR MOM'S BEST PILLOW CASES AND WHO WILL BE SO GROUNDED IF THEY GET EGG ON 'EM!
I DON'T KNOW.... WHY SHOULD I HELP YOU GUYS?
COME ON, AMELIA. HELP US OUT.
sigh
PLEASE.
YOU SELL-OUT!
you will be REWARDED!

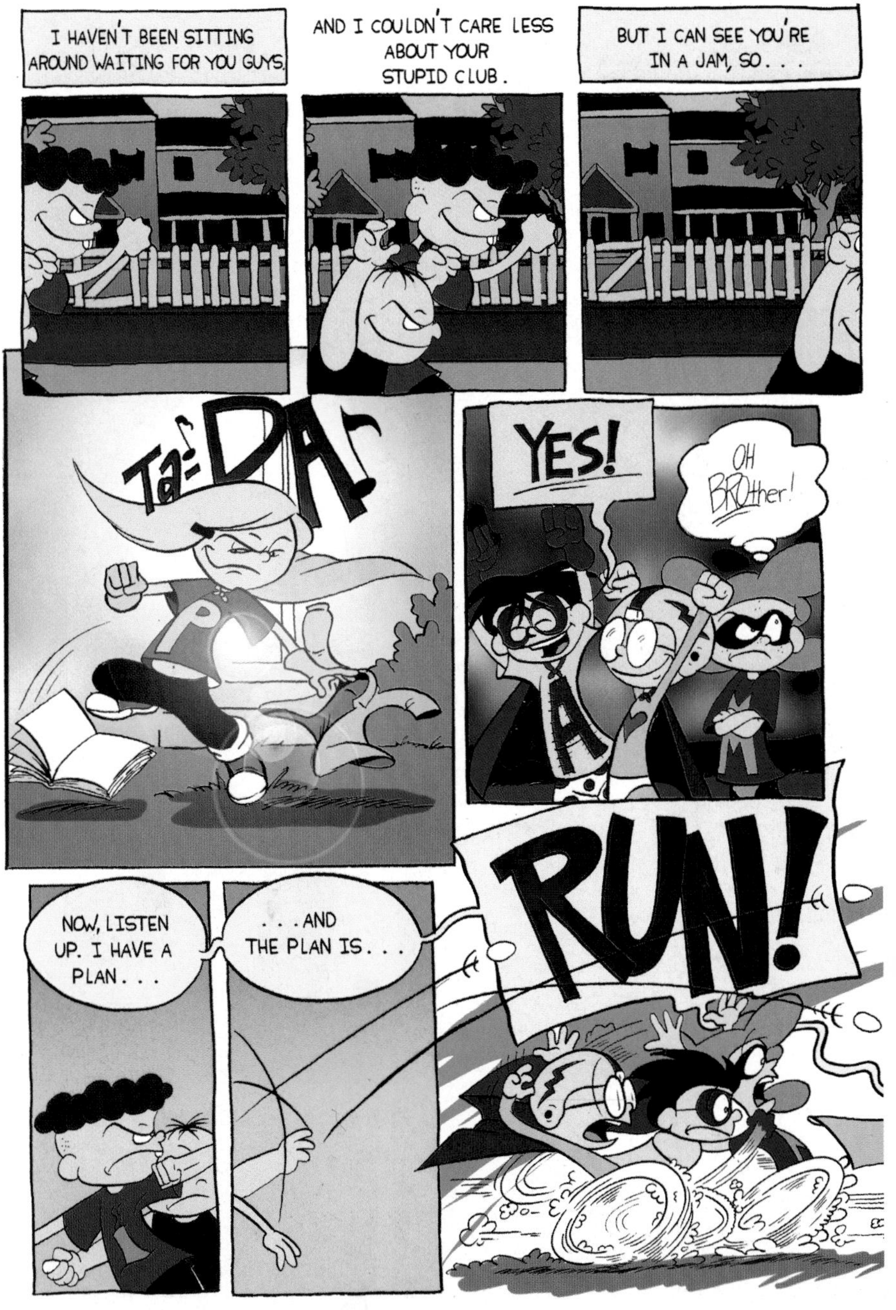
I HAVEN'T BEEN SITTING AROUND WAITING FOR YOU GUYS.
AND I COULDN'T CARE LESS ABOUT YOUR STUPID CLUB.
BUT I CAN SEE YOU'RE IN A JAM, SO . . .
Ta-DA!
YES!
OH BROther!
NOW, LISTEN UP. I HAVE A PLAN . . .
. . . AND THE PLAN IS . . .
RUN!

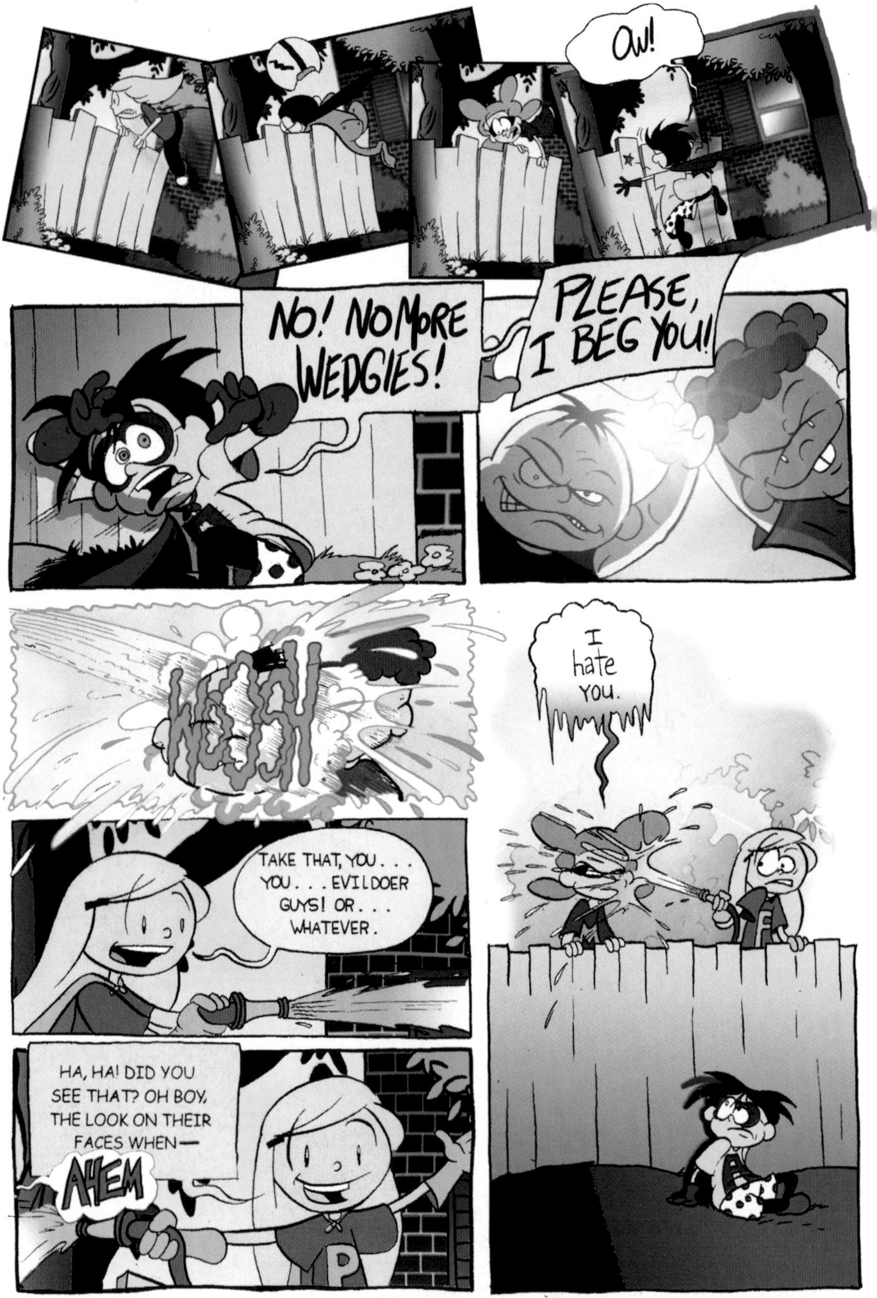
OW!
NO! NO MORE WEDGIES!
PLEASE, I BEG YOU!
WOOSH
TAKE THAT, YOU . . . YOU . . . EVILDOER GUYS! OR. . . WHATEVER.
I hate you.
HA, HA! DID YOU SEE THAT? OH BOY, THE LOOK ON THEIR FACES WHEN—
AHEM

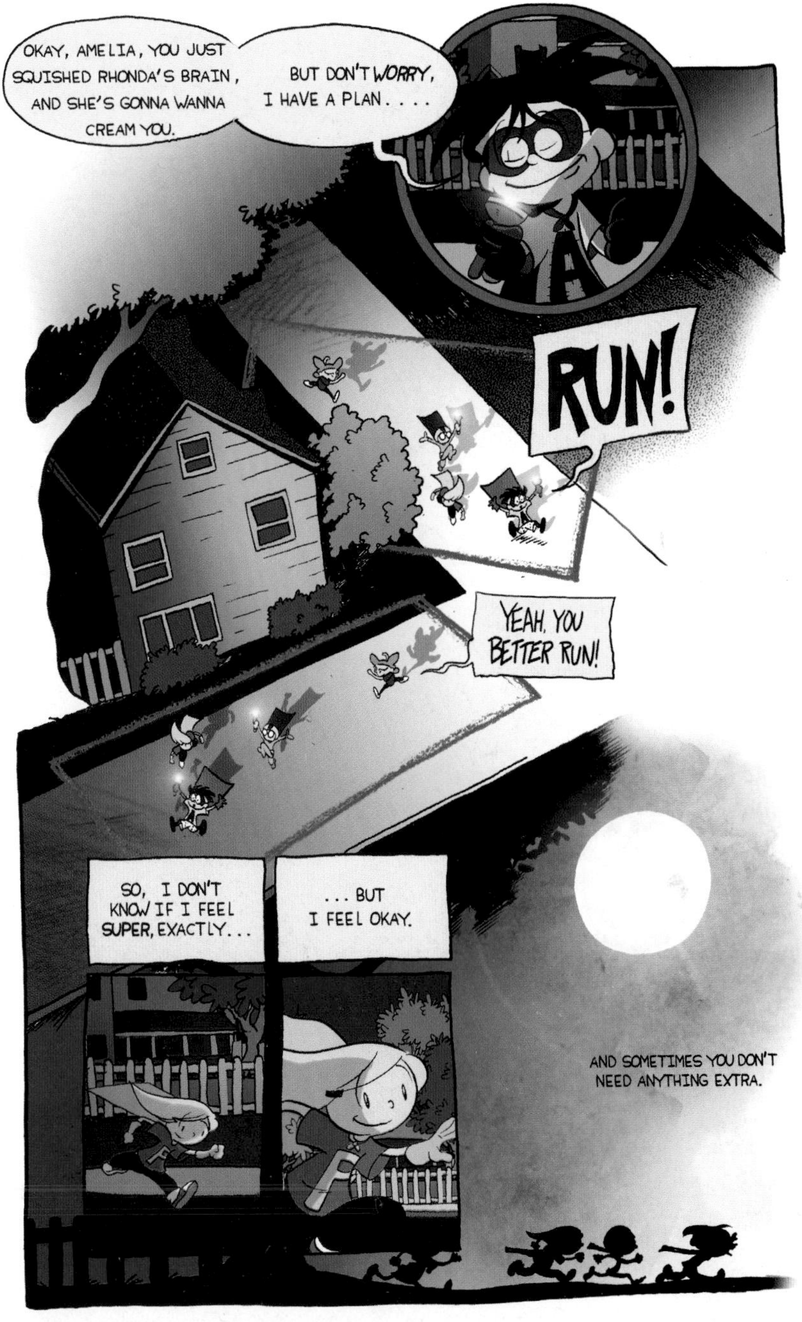
OKAY, AMELIA, YOU JUST SQUISHED RHONDA'S BRAIN, AND SHE'S GONNA WANNA CREAM YOU.
BUT DON'T WORRY, I HAVE A PLAN. . . .
RUN!
YEAH, YOU BETTER RUN!
SO, I DON'T KNOW IF I FEEL SUPER, EXACTLY...
... BUT I FEEL OKAY.
AND SOMETIMES YOU DON'T NEED ANYTHING EXTRA.

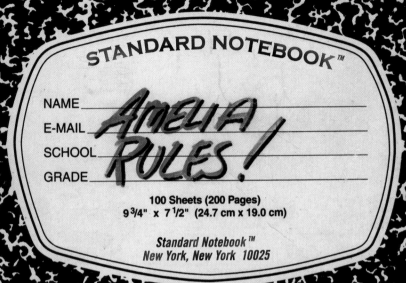

STANDARD NOTEBOOK™

NAME_____
E-MAIL_____
SCHOOL_____
GRADE_____

AMELIA RULES!

100 Sheets (200 Pages)
9 3/4" x 7 1/2" (24.7 cm x 19.0 cm)

Standard Notebook™
New York, New York 10025

Pg 7

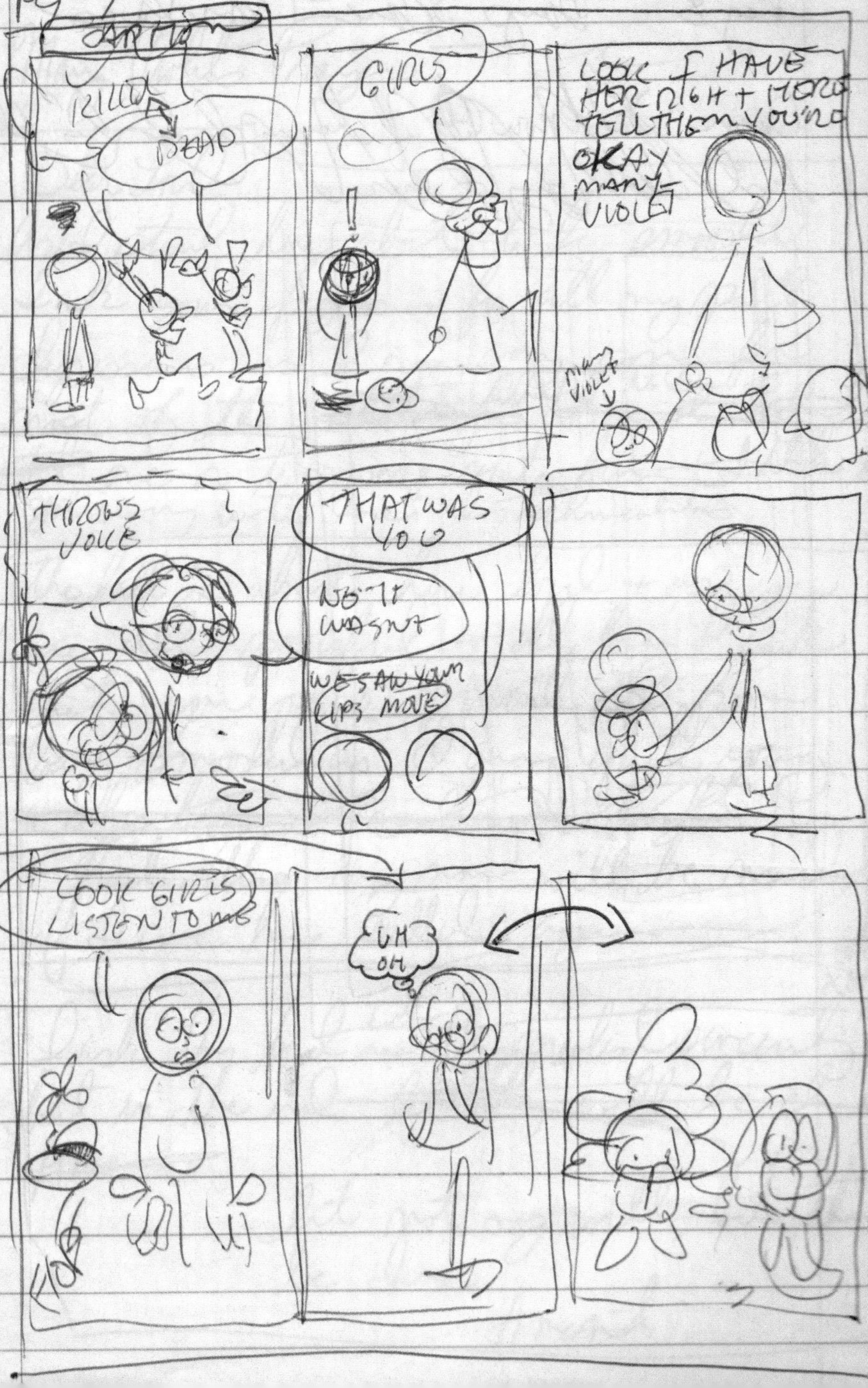
KILL
DEAD
GIRLS
LOOK I HAVE HER RIGH + HERE TELL THEM YOU'RE OKAY MARY VIOLET
MARY VIOLET
THROWS VOICE
THAT WAS YOU
NO IT WASN'T
WE SAW YOUR LIPS MOVE
LOOK GIRLS LISTEN TO ME
UH OH

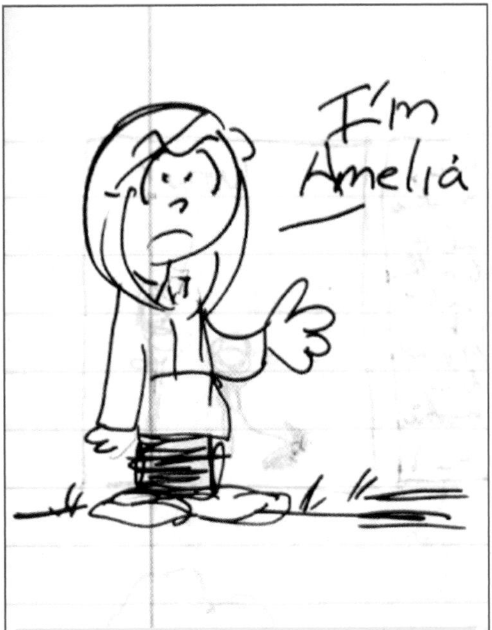
I'm Amelia
An early sketch of Amelia McBride

Every Amelia story starts in a plain old notebook.
Composition books are always my favorite, but I also carry small pocket notebooks to jot down ideas as they come to me. And I never type up scripts for my stories. Partly because I'm the world's worst typist, but also because it's a comic, so I often start with the pictures and work up the dialog later. A comic can be many things, but it should always be fun to look at. If the page is complex or if I have something very specific in mind, I'll "work it out" in my trusty notebook, as I did here (*left*) in this early draft from *The Whole World's Crazy.*

When I was first developing the Amelia Rules! series, I made sketches of each character. Some, like Amelia (*above*), didn't change very much, but others are almost unrecognizable.

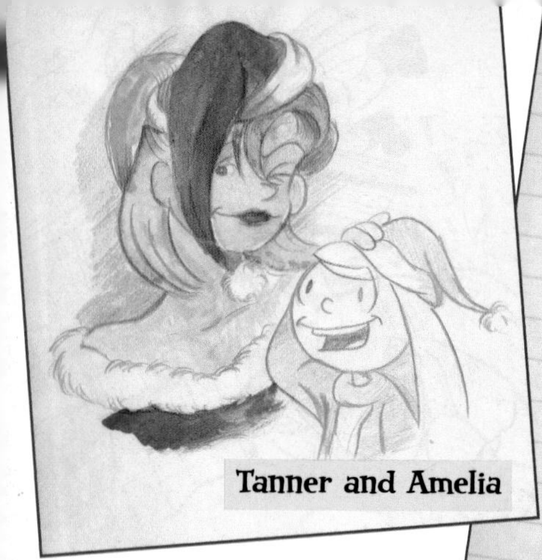

Tanner and Amelia

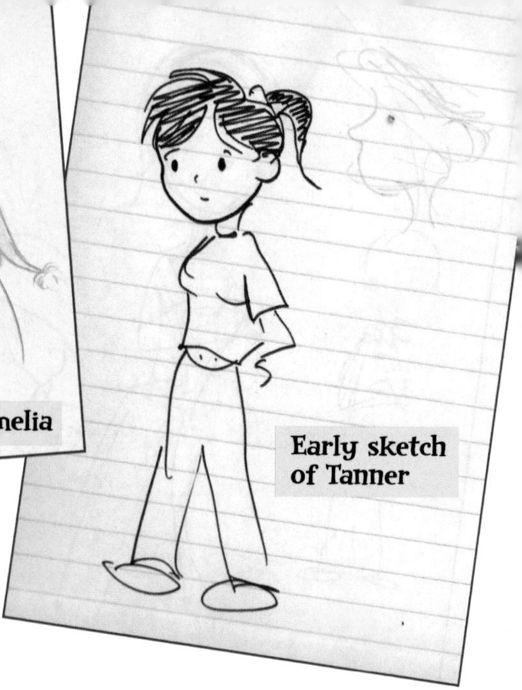

Early sketch of Tanner

Sometimes it's fun to do a drawing of your story before you even start to work, as it gives you a place from which you can draw inspiration. This is a sketch (*above*) I did before working on "The Other Side of Yuletide," and check out an early version of Rhonda (*below*)!

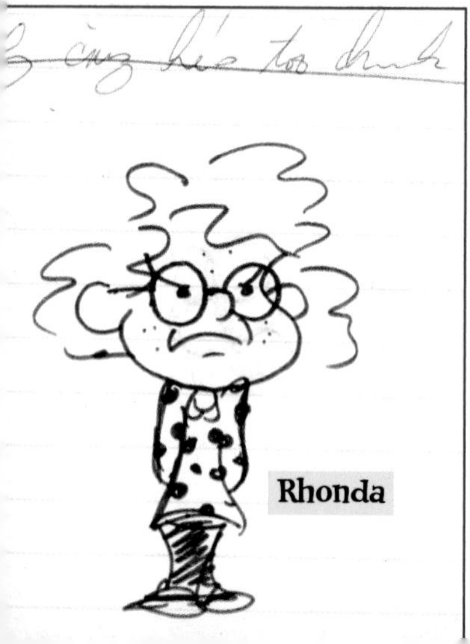

Rhonda

***Facing page*: Creating a finished comics page is a multistep process. First the page is drawn in pencil. I use mechanical pencils with 2H-graphite lead. Then the entire page is gone over in ink. For inking, I use a Zebra ultrafine brush pen for about 90 percent of the work. A crow-quill pen or a technical pen are used for details. Where are the words? Back when I was drawing this page from *What Makes You Happy*, I was using a computerized font for the lettering. These days, I'm back to doing all my lettering by hand.**

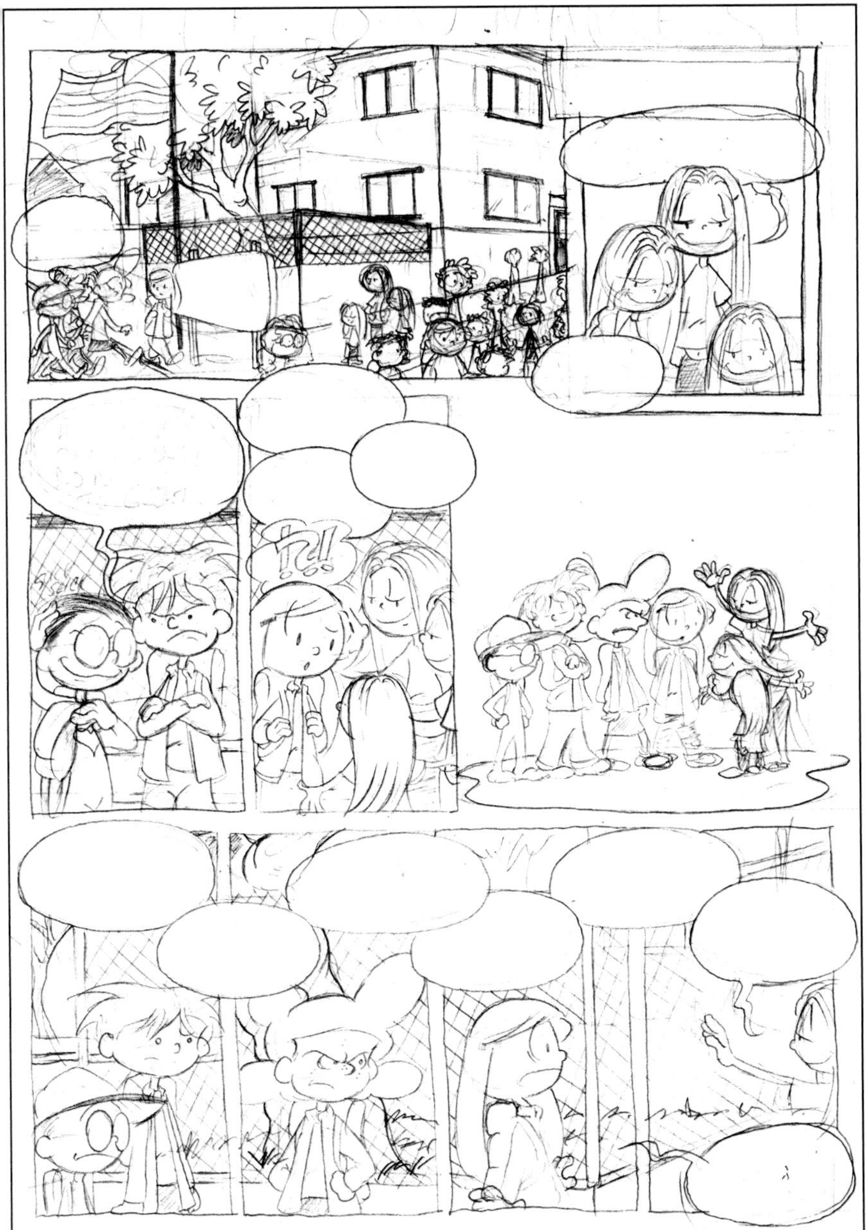

?!!

Page from *What Makes You Happy*

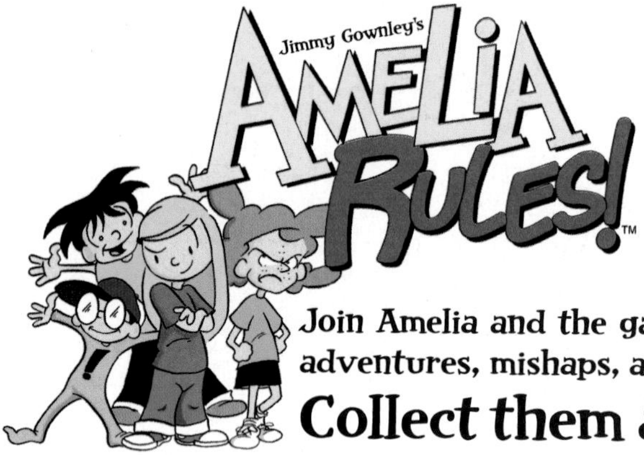
Jimmy Gownley's
AMELIA
RULES!

Join Amelia and the gang for adventures, mishaps, and homework.

Collect them all!

☐ **#1:** *The Whole World's Crazy*

ISBN: 978-1-4169-8604-1

ISBN: 978-1-4169-8606-5

☐ **#4:** *When the Past Is a Present*

Coming January 2010!

ISBN: 978-1-4169-8607-2

☐ **#5:** *The Tweenage Guide to Not Being Unpopular*

Coming April 2010!

ISBN: 978-1-4169-8610-2 (hc)
ISBN: 978-1-4169-8608-9 (pbk)